Sorrow

Stories and Poems To Read While Dead

By John Turi

Mike,
Shut up and
Read the Book!
Love
John Turi

Published Through
www.MEDIUMRAREBOOKS.com
2002

These stories are works of fiction. Names, characters, places and incidents are either the product of the author's imagination or are used fictiously. Any resemblance to actual events or locales or persons, living or dead, is entirely coincidental.

Published by Medium Rare Books
www.MediumRareBooks.com
Cover by the infamous Christopher Bloom

International Serial Book Number
ISBN 0-9711162-1-0 softcover

Manufactured in the United States of America and distributed to the book trade by www.MEDIUMRAREBOOKS.com

1 3 5 7 9 10 8 6 4 2

First Edition

Dedicated To The Only Woman
Who Figured Out How To Love Me

Shawn-Marie

Also to Jay Leno & Conan O'Brien
for keeping me sane as the writing
crept into the late night hours

- AUTHOR'S PREFACE -

I have finally put a collection of my work together, so thank you for buying and or stealing it. You will enjoy it. This project has been a magical ride thus far and by leaving these pages to the masses, some, not all, but some of the sufferings from within my crazy mixed up mind stay behind and the rest will be dealt with by my two (2) shrinks.

This collection is pretty much an unpublished collection. There were a couple that showed up on the Internet and in print, but either I forgot where or I was just dreaming the whole crazy thing.

The stories and poems inside these pages embark from a place that is inevitable to all beings: suffering. One way or another these pages tackle the desolation and wretched levels of humanity in which my mind often goes.

The following people in no particular order I would like to thank for either their help or inspiration: Momma and Poppa Turi (for the adoption), Mom and Dad Dudley (for their daughter), Dr. Mark Borg (for the memories), Mike Dalla (for the espionage), Harry Shannon (for the sanity), the Venerable Thích Cho'n Thành (for the compassion), Reverend Kusala (for the help with Jizo), Michele, Sam, Emmy, Alex Antonaras (for the family), Ron and Penny (for the spiritual talks), Ellen Jane, all of her family and a few people who never need to be named, but know who they are.

John Turi
Locked in a small padded room
with a computer and cigarettes.
September 2001

- ContentS -

~Short Stories of Sorrow~

~Poetry Of Sorrow~

“War is the great scavenger of thought.”
Sir Edmund Gosse

Lions Sleep Tonight

Part I

At the same time my index finger pulled the trigger on the AR-15 and hollowed the skull of an attacking V.C., my feet sensed the warm urine fill my boots. As the splattered gray matter of the Viet Cong landed in the tall razor grass, I shat myself. The need to vomit out a scream came next. It was terror, escaping from every opening I had. Before today, I've never killed anyone.

Seven minutes after Charlie finished his ambush, the rain-soaked jungle became quiet. I had a pile in my pants and my boots swooshed as I crouched down and waited. "Never trust the quiet in the jungle after an ambush, they told us in boot camp. That's the perfect time for the Gooks to fuck you!"

I listened and waited. Not a sound, even the tigers were quiet. Fear, more than patience, held me against the bamboo tree. My company was a half click down the hill from Nha Trang. Our objective: Destroy a covert harbor that was the main transporter for the NLF. This was a central route for the NLF to bring in anti-aircraft rockets from the Gulf of Tonkin. Our intelligence informed us that these rockets could be used to bomb American embassies in Qui Nhon, Tuy Hoa and Saigon.

The radio on Marrow's backpack was squawking. I could not make out who was talking over it, but I wished they would have shut up. It was their voice that was disturbing the silence in the jungle. As long as there was silence I felt calm.

"Flash Delta, this is Op. Nine-Five-Seven. What is your stat? Over?" The radio kept repeating that over and over. I could not move over to Marrow to answer the radio. His head was ripped off his shoulders and had been held on by the radio receiver cord; it made me sick to look at him. I tossed my 9" hunting knife at the radio, to shut it off. I missed; it stuck into Marrow's boot. I was tired, scared and I peed my pants just to relax. If I ignored the radio maybe they would come for us-for me? I sat still and sang quietly to myself.

Black humor made me sing: "In the jungle the mighty jungle…"

Gunfire brought the jungle back screaming. Wind from a bullet coming north grazed my ear. It sounded like a swarm of bees attacking as it went by and lodged into a bamboo tree. I crouched, scurried and felt the load in my pants slide around up part of my back and stick to my shirt. I ripped off my shirt and moved away from the tree. I had to get moving, they were close. My naked belly slid across the wet jungle floor and over the remains of Jones. He was the black kid from Mississippi. He was-had been-nineteen. The warm smooth texture of his intestines against my stomach felt comforting, like holding a baby right after it had left the womb. If these bodies were not recovered by a support squad, the tigers would devour them at dawn.

A mortar went off ten yards behind me. I felt the searing shrapnel scratch my head. My helmet stopped the debris from cracking my skull. Even though there was blood dripping down my face, I felt I was okay; I just needed to keep moving. Charlie was advancing and I didn't think I could hold them off any longer.

I rested against another tree and grabbed a box of Camels off of Rodriguez's helmet. My hands shook as I tried to light one. Good old Zippos, they never fail when you need them. The first inhale of that wonderful smoke was like a shot of morphine. I looked around the wet jungle and saw my company frozen in awkward positions, all dead or dying. More gunfire. This time from the north and east. The V.C. were getting closer. Another drag of the Camel. More bullets, a grenade, too far away to get me. I felt light headed from the Camel. I heard Gook chatter. It was Charlie; he was all around me. I needed to hide, run, but there was no time for escape. I pushed the Camel in the dirt and slid my body under Rodriguez. He was colder than Jones, not as comforting. The blood from Rodriguez's mouth dripped. It nagged me like a leaky faucet on a sleepless night. I took some of the coagulated blood from his jaw and rubbed it against my face. I wanted to hide my whiteness. Dizzy, I closed my eyes. I passed out as Charlie strolled into the area to finish off the wounded.

Part II

Sun faded covers of *Time, Life* and *National Geographic* on the bench next to me. Interesting articles and pictures torn out of the stapled bindings, months before I had a chance to see what had been so interesting.

Dust slowly whispered in from under the main door at the Greyhound Bus Terminal. The man behind the counter had just announced that the next bus would be arriving in four minutes. An elderly couple sat across from me. The gray hairs of the woman stole out from under her summer hat. Her face was soft, serene. She waved away the dust that blew around her with her wrinkled copy of *Time*. Her husband looked comfortable sleeping on her shoulder. His belly and wrinkled face relaxed; scarred hands, worn from many years of hard labor, curled like talons. He was probably a dirt-scrabble farmer like my dad. I wondered how long these two had been married. Does a duet of so many years twist you tightly together? So close that death will be the only separation you can know?

The main door opened. Magazines flew open and danced about. The bus had arrived. I left the rest of my thoughts stacked with the cluttered magazines, there for the next lonely soldier to examine. I grabbed my duffel bag and walked out into the hot Oklahoma sunshine.

Seven other people, besides myself and the couple from the terminal. The bus ride, for me, would be eight hours and forty-three minutes. We stopped five times along the way. On two of those five stops I got off: Once to use the restroom, the second time to stretch my legs and feel the fresh air scorch my lungs. Dry air, totally unlike the humid jungle I had left behind only nine days ago.

I watched the sun set across a wheat field that rolled as far as the eye could see. It was one of the most beautiful vistas I had ever seen. Orange blazed through the field like an inferno, with fiery rubies and scarlet smoke blending into rows of wheat and shadows. I sat with my face pressed against the dusty bus, window marveling at the sheer beauty, trying to let it erase the horror that reflects in my mind like a sideshow mirror.

Darkness crept in like a ghost, and the stale air began suffocating our breath. Some us tried to sleep. Miles and miles of flat land disappeared into the night, bringing billions of stars into immediacy, as if intended to remind us of God's brilliance. The same stars that most of my battalion glanced at in silence, as we waited in our muddy foxholes. We had gazed at those bright stars and wondered which family member or girlfriend was sharing them with us from back in the real world. My eyes watched the stars until my eye lids grew heavy. I slept the rest of the ride and awoke when the bus stopped at the next terminal.

In my deep, deep sleep I dreamed the vivid and colorful dreams of my childhood. Walks in the snow with Zephyr, our family German shepard. We'd had him for as long as I could remember. Sneaking cigarettes from my grandfather's pocket as he slept. Then running behind the barn with Mitchell Gregory and Mark Grover, my two best friends. We tried inhaling the smoke, but all we did was cough and choke. We laughed at each other as we turned green. Once, by accident, we lit the brush surrounding the barn and it burst into flames. We peed frantically on the blaze to put the fire out before my father saw the smoke. It worked, and he never knew.

In my deep dreams, I felt my first kiss. Little Marianne Grover; I was fourteen and she was twelve. I brushed her soft skin with my trembling hands. While placing my lips against hers, I felt her probing tongue. My knees shook, and I wanted to hide from the world after that. She and her brother Mark had waved goodbye to me as I left on the bus for 'Nam. In one of Mom's letters, she'd told me that Mark was killed in a car accident off of I-33. He fell asleep, they said. That was almost two years ago.

The dreams brought me to the summer when I was sixteen. I was down at the watering hole with a bunch of kids from school. I was showing off and hung upside down on the old tree swing, swaying back and forth until the bough broke. I fell six feet to the ground and cracked my head open. My mother sewed my broken scalp back together that night. As she slid the thread in and out of my skin, looping back and forth with a needle that was sterilized from a match, she hummed to me the "Jungle Song". The thread stung and tickled my scalp, sending chills down my neck. I dreamed away a life gone by on that bus ride. I never felt more at peace before in my entire life.

Part III

The bright morning sun hit me like a sledge hammer, fracturing my dreams and spilling my boyhood memories all over the road. I grabbed my bag and walked into the bus terminal. This one had the same sun-faded magazines, stale candy and flat pop machines as the last one. I was deep in Oklahoma. When you're this far inside everything starts looking the same. Flat land for miles and miles, dirt, weeds, road kill, dust, and plenty of sunshine. It was good to be almost home. I couldn't have handled another tour in the jungle, being knee deep in mud as snakes moved along with you, exploding grenades echoing all day in your head, wild cross fire whizzing all around; and as you sleep - always a very light sleep because the helicopters flew close enough for you to read the dog tags around the pilots' neck

Moving from the back of the line to the front line. That was always the objective: Kill or be killed. As you'd press forward you'd step on pieces of enemies and allies. Trying to figure out which was a problem. Everyone looked the same from the inside out and the stench of decomposing soldiers burned you back into your sanity.

One time our squad advanced from two clicks down a secured outpost, up to an unsettled river that had a name you could never pronounce. A river heavily trapped and wired. Our Gunny told us to be on the lookout, check in all directions for the V.C. But they hid in the bushes and dug and camouflaged holes and tunnels. We always had to watch where we stepped. Live wires and booby traps would remove limbs and turn young bodies into hamburger. "And that shit don't come off your boot when you step on it. It's like dog shit, just sticks there," Gunny said. A harsh world. 'Nam was not my idea of fun.

The last reeking bus pulled up, the final ride home for me. Two more hours and I'd be back with my folks. Back in the town where I learned to walk, talk, drive, fish, read, and write. Mom would have a special supper ready: turkey with all the fixings and hot apple pie cooling on the window sill. My room would be as I left it, my baseball trophies dusted and shined. Dad would l have my Plymouth tuned up and ready for me to drive into town where my buddies, the ones who made it back to the world, would be waiting for me.

The highway sign read: Denton, Oklahoma 3 miles. Home was near. I could see the smoke from the slaughter house blowing to the north. I could almost smell the hot apple pie. Come on, bus driver, hurry up! Don't you know that I haven't been home in two and a half years? I served my country and protected my nation. I killed those communist murderers. My family has missed me. Marianne Grover might want to see me. My dog will be wagging his tail waiting for me; he knows I'm coming home. I'm going where I belong. Where I'll raise my children and they'll raise theirs. Drive faster! I want to get home and sleep in my bed. Do you know how long it has been since I've slept on freshly washed sheets? I want to hug my mom and dad. I want to tell them that this was not like the war dad fought in, not at all. This war was savage, and it didn't mean shit or change anything. I saw things that I would rather forget. Things I don't want to think about. Hurry up driver! I've had my life placed on hold long enough. I'm ready to start living again. Living normal, just like everyone else.

Part IV

I arrived in Denton at 16:30 hours April 10, 1966. My mother was there to greet me. Her blue eyes hid behind tears, and her hair had gone a little gray. She was still as beautiful as I remembered. Father was composed, like a veteran soldier. His pain hid behind his well-trained eyes. It was my father who took the clipboard from the bus driver, lifted the pen, and signed his name. He marked on the form that verified my arrival. The form that declared that in the coffin at his feet lay the body of his son.

The flag at Denton City Hall flew at half mass the next morning. That afternoon I was buried next to my grandfather at Hillsgrove cemetery. The entire town was there to mourn me. The Veteran's Hall laid an American flag over my coffin and handed it to my sobbing mother. Marianne Grover did come. She held Zephyrs leash; his tail had stopped wagging.

After the funeral there was a potluck at the Lutheran church. Everyone brought something homemade. Mom made two apple pies, but no one ate much. Mrs. Gregory sat alone in a folding chair outside. She rocked and cried. Reverend Daniel's comforted her as best he could. But like mom she, too, would be burying her only son come Friday.

My buddy Mitchell Gregory was enjoying his last bus ride home from the jungle, the mighty jungle where all of us lions sleep tonight.

Last 1-2-C-U

(The vim and vigor of a mortician)

Throat!
That was where I began the first assault on you
You came to me dead to the world
Lying on your back, still warm
Clothed in only a sheet soaked in damp morning's dew
Droplets that ran from your body as they elevated
You off from the bitter ground
In peace you remain waiting for me
To fill you with chemicals for their satisfaction
Into your throat the device penetrates
Away your color drains into the open waiting world
Will you miss them, remember them or love them
Let me hold your hand, arms, feet, ankles, legs
To circulate your blood I have just become your heart
They will be here to see you soon
I must make you beautiful for them
For it is their only chance to say goodbye

Recipe For Infinity

How elevated your temperature is as I bake your heart
In-side the fire of neglected security
Burning on an open flame for the world to smell
Your suffering drips like gristle on the floor
Stupidity is not the final ingredient, mind you
The final ingredient is the craving for more
I cannot, will not, must not serve you up to the world
You are mine alone, so the Bible tells me
Let them find their own recipe
The only thing I can consume is you
So why bake your heart in the fire of apprehension?
Because long ago, I presume this recipe for infinity
Was passed down to me
From one family member to the next
And all it said was:
1 cup of a person you would die for
2 tablespoons of lack of trust
3 pinches of scent of another woman
Bake on an open fire until it leaves
When I see you next, after you have sat on the
Window sill and cooled a while
Remind me to make chocolate chip cookies instead
Of your heart, our love and my fears
For the world to smell and savor

"There is no psychology; there is
only biography and autobiography."
Thomas Szasz

Recollection

There is an area on the edge of the brain called lunacy. This place is the divided world of make believe and the thoughts to distinguish. Again and again, perception is the root that is uniquely altered. Never mother-fucking ever let them tell you it is not! I've seen so many things in life and have listened to so many people suffering and dying and yet, unforgettably, all I can do is perceive them for who they are as my thoughts. In my reality much different than their own, I see these thoughts as I see probability. The chance of loneliness, fear, and most of all, the chance to suffer from repeated life given tortures: Memories.

Most times these denied chances haunt like a bad dream in the night. I'm sorry, but this is the real world. This is how we live amongst each other. This how you watch television, how you cry under your pillow, remembering the days of spooked-up yesterdays.

You are about to embark on a little journey through my perception of how I see people and more importantly, how I treat them. Now sit back and try and recall those days way back in your memory of a time called youth. But always remember whatever you are thinking or feeling, it is coming from my observation, where nothing is simple. In my world you never sleep. In my world we die alone. In my world there is no such thing as a cure for suffering.

We sat across from one another in my office. I've known her for a short time: three weeks, to be exact. Speaking of me, I would have to say that I do get inside people easily. I'm a comfortable man, if I do say so myself. For that reason it was easy for her to open up to me. She opened way up; I could see down her throat from where I sat and watched her heart pulse. Her back was against the window as the sun peered through her sundress. The time was 1:20 in the afternoon. My calendar with the month of May crossed out all the way to the 15th was present. I was noticing these things while she talked to me. I tried, Oh' I tried paying attention, but I wandered a bit. I couldn't help it. Not sure why? Maybe it was the intensity of her voice as she spoke to me in a calm familiarity and then at times not many but a few she raged like a child with hyperthyroidism. But remember we are in my mind. You're all listening to her through my mind. So far this is what I have of her in my memory. These are her chances, her recollection of tragedy.

"I lived across town away from most of my friends. It was still Long Beach. And it was a nice-looking house. But it was a small quiet house where kids played by themselves in their own yards." This is how she started a moment in her life. My mind saw different. My mind took in what you will envision also. It is much better, really, than listening to this boring blabbermouth babble tiresomely on about her deplorable life.

Yellow faded paint peeled from the exterior of a slum-warped dwelling. The interior had a drunken father sprawled on the couch burping and farting at the television, the only furnishings around the whole household. Budweiser beer cans littered the living room; some were on the coffee table other near it. Dried up beer foam ran its' way down the leg of the coffee table and onto the rug; a faded Dacron carpet, at one time eggshell white, now the color of weather worn dog waste. A new Sony stereo stood next to the fireplace, a fake brick hearth that housed fake logs: worthless piece of art that somehow added to the texture of the dwelling. Speakers all by themselves sat on both sides of the couch. MTV poured out of the television and the stereo. Two units hooked up as one: multiple noise inflexibility. The sounds of unwanted laughing children only twenty-five feet away went unheard. This woman sitting across from me was one of the children. I am not sure how old; she has not specified, I am imaging ten years old. Actually I could give a shit at this point. I was having trouble listening to her babble on and on about her life.

My head listened in its sorted destructive manner. Her output of thoughts into my input conception was untamed. This is how I pictured her talking nonsense… A woman singing in the kitchen cooked dinner, trying every means possible to drown out the noise of MTV in the other room. She did the best she could at raising her voice level high enough and still being able to concentrate on her work. Actually she had good practice at shouting all of her life. Everyone marries his or her own father or mother. Well, that's what her mother used to tell her.

I'm listening to her speak to me. Her voice is calm right now. It's soothing in some sick way. She is still talking about the woman in the kitchen, her mother. So now my head goes inside her mother's thoughts, from inside my interpretation of her is probably not far from the truth.

Wendy Bryant thought more of her life before children and a drunken farting husband. She was a dancer in Germany during Vietnam; she danced at a cocktail club on an Army base in Breminhaven. A Go-Go bar they used to be called in the 1960's, a disco during the '70', a singles bar in the '80's and a basic nightclub during the '90's.

She looked fine, long tan legs hiding in vinyl boots that reached up above her kneecaps. The boots were made for dancing - on tables. But then that is when the fun started to stop; she took her dancing more as a career rather than a hobby since she left the states in search of herself.

How she ended up in Breminhaven is another story that she does not want to ponder. But her choices to find a soldier were dying down, as the base was deploying most of its infantry to Vietnam. She still believed in the power of the Feminist movement back in the states, but that was so far away. German women succumbed to a secluded lifestyle. Her energy was running low, as was the money, the nerves, and the reason why she came to be dancer. Wendy needed to eat and needed to keep her child from dying; the child that had been growing only a month in her belly. She needed a man to take her away from all this, all of the drunken brawls and drunken dates. The last date turned out to be more than she expected.

Wendy begged for them to stop, but soldiers will be primal during war. A total of nineteen service men took her out back behind the bar while she was passed out in the storage area from dancing and drinking for nine hours. They split her purple miniskirt in half - like plucking a feather from a dead chicken. A private by the name of Anderson hit her mouth; blood ran down onto her breast. He held a 9" hunting knife to her throat. That much she remembered, that much still is visible in her thoughts. That small scar on her upper lip still screams at her: Remember me, Wendy! Remember your secret! Her memory cries on and on. It could have been hours or days later when she woke up and semen mixed with blood dripped from her vagina resembling Mr. Bubble Bath Soap, a color of liquid that her children would become familiar with as they grew up.

Abortion was a scary thing in the 1960's and even more in another country. Wendy kept the child that was forced upon her. One out of nineteen men was the father and she vowed never to tell anyone of this experience. Shortly after that he walked in and swooped her off those vinyl boots. It only took three weeks and the boots were retired to a pair of slippers and Wendy was living in another country, a familiar country. Finally she was away from the memories abroad, but not away from the drunken brawls. Remember what Momma said, Wendy: "We always marry are fathers." That is true. Didn't your father drink when you were young? Wasn't he also the first one who made pink liquid drip from your cunt? He loved you, you fucking whore! Again and again you messed up your life and now this woman sitting across from me is jabbering about it. Why didn't you just shove a rusty coathanger up your twat and rip this woman in front of me out?

You could of tossed her fetus in an alley and let the pigeons dine on her. Then I could be out playing a nice nine holes before my afternoon meeting. You selfish fucking tramp!

I stood up and my patient, who we will call Anna, stopped talking. I cracked a nice smile and asked her if she needed something to drink. I lit her cigarette and opened the little refrigerator. I gave her a glass of water in a Tom & Jerry jelly glass and plopped three ice cubes in it. I kissed her on her forehead. She shrunk back a little, and I returned to my seat that was still warm. I looked at her and said, "Proceed, please." She smiled and continued.

They rented a house on Hamburg Street in Long Beach. The rent was cheap and the owners of the house were nice. They trusted the young parents. They trusted them to look after the house and take care of the place. Fix it up, so to speak: Never happened.

Anna continued on about her mom. As I refocused my thought of what her mother was thinking. Yes, the work would be light, Mathew would help out after all and she was carrying his baby in her belly. A lie that she would take to the grave, a fabrication worse than anything a woman could do in her entire life. But she needed a change and this man was the right person to do it, so she thought.

"Wendy get me another beer!" A staggered yell shouted over MTV.

Wendy came back from Fantasy World. Wendy, get this, Wendy get that. Wendy, clean this house and make me dinner. Fuck you! Her mind hailed from Anna's mind into my mind and now into your mind.

"Mommy, what time's dinner?" A child peaked in

through the front screen door, a tiny spot of screen dirt laid on her nose. Behind her an older sister sat, not her true sister but they never knew it.

"In a little bit, hon. You and your sister come in and get cleaned up." Smiling children with smiling dirt on their face walked past the farting burping blob on the couch.

"Hi, dad?" Little Anna whispered in a puzzled voice. This was not the father she knew and loved or was it? She can only remember a few times when dad wasn't half crocked on Budweiser after work. But he never had a problem like those bums she saw in the alleys, he just liked to relax. Wake up, Anna, you're all grown-up now and still think your old man is still relaxing. I was getting sleepy. I tried listening to her, but I was losing it. This is where my head goes a bit insane.

"Here's your beer, Mat. Can you get the next one yourself, please, I'm trying to finish dinner!" The words came out harder than expected, a rebuttal was do any second.

"Fuck you, I work hard all day and all you do is play with the kids and talk on the Goddamn phone!"

"Mat, please don't start with me, I have a headache!" Two children placed their ears against the bathroom door and listened to the usual yelling.

"There're at it again, Susan." A few tears fell from Anna's eye, as they did in front of me. I watched them fall onto the table; I hoped they did not dry until after she left. I want to put them under a microscope and see what lies within their foundation.

"I know, it must have been Dad's fault." The same sides where taken when a fight broke out at the Bryant household. Susan, Anna's younger sister by two years, always grabbed moms side, while Anna defended her father who was not a drunk, despite what the neighbors said.

"Anna, Susan come on!" A voice trying to be sober called from the couch.

The two wiped their hands off on the blue bathroom

towel and stepped out of the room. The feeling these two kids got was like entering a haunted house at a carnival. You never know when the Boogey man will jump out and get you.

"Come on, we're going out." The Boogey man eyed his wifes, as she brandished a kitchen knife behind her back.

"You leave this house and I'll destroy all of your shit! Do you hear me?" The scream came from atop the porch, neighbors watched but without directly looking at the scene. The neighborhood was used to this and had ignored it for ten years.

"Where are we going Daddy?" Susan piped up from the back seat of the Jeep CJ-7.

"I'm hungry. Let's stop at Bull-n-Bun and get a burger!" Anna's little chubby cheeks smiled up at her father. I guess Anna was fat when she was young. But her cocaine habit for the last five years has depleted all of that weight. The doctor said she would outgrow it in a few years. Never happened, until she whored her body around town, and shoved shit up her nose. Why am I still listening to this woman? She is just like her mother and will end up like her mother. I can't help her. But I listened anyway. I didn't have anything to do until three.

"We'll eat and let your mother cool off a while. We're going to your uncle's house for a few hours." Anna's spine crept a chill. A chill crept through Anna's spine a deep haunting chill that a lot of little boys and girl get. Most of who come and talk to shrinks like me when their older and more scared of moving onward in life. These people suffer from low self-esteem, suicidal tendencies, prostitution and similar traumas. Anna had been hiding for the past five years, she didn't know any better and who was the wiser. If she told anyone, her mommy would die, so she was told. Uncle Ronald lived in a big house in Cerritos. He made his money selling used cars for Ford, down at the Auto Square. But he made his nuts explode touching little children.

"Do we have to go to Uncle Ron's?" Anna cried.

"He will be glad to see you guys, and Mom really needs to cool down. We'll eat in a little while." Mat smiled lightly at his little girl.

Anna sat quietly in the front seat as her mind wandered back on the last visit to Uncle Ron's. He was watching her and her little sister. Mom and Dad went to a movie and no baby-sitter was available. Ronald was glad to watch them and whatever else came up.

This I found interesting. I often would sit up late at night and think to myself what it takes to rape a small child. Take off their clothes and fondle them. I wonder how deranged you have to be in order to did that and live with yourself. How did it feel to rub and fondle smooth baby fresh skin? It disgusted me, the thought of such perversion. I have had a few pedophiles that have come to see me and I would prescribe them wrong medications and pray they go insane. Two have committed suicide and I double billed their insurance companies for wasting my time.

Anna went on. I refreshed her water and she lit her own cigarette. I lit one too. My mind went deeper, and I heard this…

Mathew and Wendy left just ten minutes ago, when Ronald decided to play a game with the children.

"Let's spin the bottle, girls!" he cried in a childish talk, the kind a small boy does when he wants to know what is behind door number one or little skirt number two.

Ron kept on kissing his nieces and Anna felt a little funny. She walked over on the couch and watch as her sister started to bleed between her legs. A fear raced in her and she thought her Uncle was stabbing her sister with a knife between his legs. She cried inside and wondered if she was next, but in a way she didn't mind. She liked the attention

Susan was getting and became a little jealous. Despite Susan's caterwauling Anna wanted to be stabbed.

I listened to this, not interpreting my own imagination as she talked. I was listening to her and I wished you could see her expression, like a child at Disneyland. She had placed her hands in between her legs and rocked back and forth. Her voice was child like, almost a quiver. My God! She was getting hysterical. This was beautiful. I was amazed at this. I wish I had a camera, good thing I was audio taping this.

It took a few minutes and Anna looked at her sister. She felt dirty, not the kind with mud and leaves, but inside dirty as her uncle bathed her and rinsed her privates. She was supposed to trust this man because he was an adult and Mom said they must never question or talk back to an adult. Pink liquid ran down her legs and Anna promised not to tell anyone. Uncle Ronald said if they told that Mom would die. Anna left that time in her life and went back to her Mom. Wendy looked around the house; for the time being her anger has stopped. No music played out of the new system and dinner sat on the table cold. A news flash shuffled past her as she flipped the television stations back and forth with the remote control.

"...and still no word on the shooting of three children in Long Beach. We asked Captain Brian Fawler what his views are on the case. He has no added comments as yet. . ." She changed the channel and saw Magnum P.I. drive a red Ferrari along a Hawaiian road. She left the station there. Dirt poured off the tires of a red Jeep CJ-7. Mat looked at his daughters, at least they smiled. They parked on the lawn, tires resting on a brown surface, a spot where grass had grown many months before the Jeep arrived. I guess this is called taking care of the house for cheap rent.

Anna and Susan jumped from the door panel, at least a two-foot distance. The CJ-7 was raised a little bit, just a portion more than standard sizes, but these children didn't care if they jumped twenty feet, they where home and life was better at home. No matter how sick it was, yelling, screaming and fighting. It was always better than being at Uncle Ronald's; he scared them, he had always scared them. But this time Uncle Ronald just sat and got drunk with his brother.

The television could be heard from the front porch: audience laughter and someone yelling. Susan walked into the house first; actually Susan stepped around things as she entered the house. Anna followed and immediately wanted to cry. The sisters stood in the dining room and glanced all around.

They almost fell down trying not to turn around. They gave a nonchalant look. Then it started all over again. Hell broke loose from the gates and Anna and Susan felt right at home.

"Wendy, what the fuck did you do?" Mathew stared at Wendy. He tried not to gaze around the room where books lay shredded on the floor. Playboy magazines pranced from the magazine rack all the way to the kitchen trash; hundreds of pages littered the floor, a gun collection that has been handed down from Great grandpa Bryant lay in splinters, Sony parts could be seen all along the fake fireplace, speaker's that once yelled MTV had what looked like a sledgehammer hole kicked through them.

"Don't look at me like that, you bastard!" She was up and Anna and her sister headed for a safe place, Susan's bedroom.

"I just want you out of this house!" Mat gave a final look at the mess strewn across the house, he was about to explode. He worked a lot of hours over time at the plant to pay for the Sony stereo and this bitch didn't appreciate anything he gives her. Should of left her in Germany to sell her cunt to the bums! Mathew stepped over the mess and pushed his wife down on the couch. He was not sure what he would do, kill her or wound her? His mind was so deranged either one would be all right.

"Touch me, and I'll kill you!" A knife came from under the cushion of the couch. A woman has to do a lot of thinking to get the details down; Wendy had had ten years of thinking and a childhood of this behavior. She knew what she had to do. Anna could hear things falling from the other side of the door. Anna held Susan tighter and the bedroom door opened.

"Girls, go outside, use your bedroom window." Wendy had a cut on her lip.

"I'm sorry mom, it's my fault!" Wendy looked at her.

"No, Anna, nothing is your fault. Just get outside and take your sister with you!" There was no use in talking the two children clung to her as is if she was the last strand of rope on a burnig bridge.

"Go outside and hide in the garage! Go!"

Susan let go first. Anna held on a bit longer and was pushed to the ground. Her butt hit the hardwood floor, and she wanted her mother to die, in that split second. Anna wished she was never born, and that her mother would die. Her sister shared the same thoughts seconds after she exited out the window.

"It's my fault that you and dad are fighting!" Anna screamed as Wendy gripped her child's arms and shoved her through the windowpane and onto a rose bush.

"Yes, it's your fault, Anna! It's you fault I'm in this country! It's your fault I was raped ten years ago! Now go in the garage!" Her face was inches away from her daughter. She yelled hoarsely at her. For a moment Wendy's only had good intentions. Anna took it all wrong and for several more years to follow, after all of the insanity that has not even started yet Anna will never forgive her mom.

The garage was cold and damp. Tires hung on the wall, tools lined the workbench and a hammer sat inside a 1969 Roadrunner another present for Dad to find. Susan thought and laughed a little. Susan hugged her sister and told her that it wasn't her fault. Mom just said that because she was mad.

"I just wish I was never born, Susan." Anna pouted and Susan shook her head.

I guess that was really all it took and that was all it ever took. Wendy walked back into the bedroom, where Mathew sat on the bed. Huffing and puffing, he was naked. The room was messed up, not as bad as the living room, but messed up enough. He grabbed his wife as she walked passed him. Despite everything they had been through and more importantly what their children were going, through, these two people fucked with wild abandon. Both had cuts and bruises on them, but they still fucked as their children sat in fear across the yard.

Anna stopped talking. The room was silent. I could hear the traffic outside my office. The bright pretty sun hid behind the clouds, like Anna's hands behind her face. Finally she looked up and told me that was all. I lost the truth between her sorrow and my lunacy. I came to the conclusion that it does not matter. Despite my efforts she is doing better. With that I stand, hugged her and could feel her breasts on my chest.

"I'll see you next week at the same time and we will discuss all of it more carefully. Also your progress is remarkable."

She smiled at me. "Oh', one more thing, I need to up your rate." She nodded and opened the door to the waiting room.

As Anna went out my front office door, my next patient sat there looking absolutely useless. I've seen Leonard twice; child abuser, alcoholic. He smiled as Anna walked by. Then turns his head towards me saying. "What's up Doc?" What a fucking queer thing to say, I mumble to myself. Leonard's features looked aged and frail. The medication was working. I glanced at the clock behind him, cringing at the thought of listening to him for fifty minutes. Today, I would increase his medication dose, because I need this time slot to relax when Anna leaves.

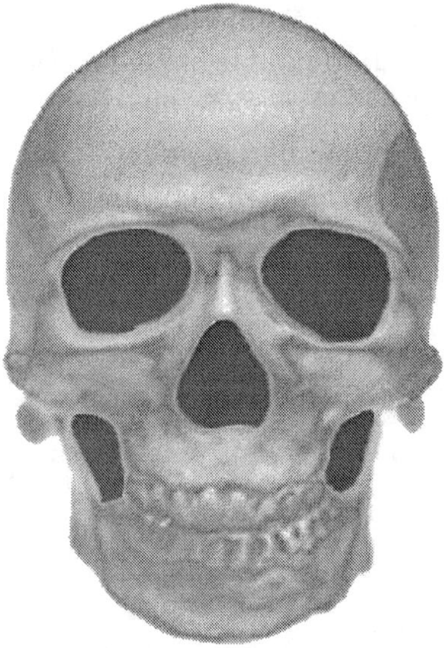

All The Way Down

Yell from within your essence –
Over and over again
Under flesh and over bone
Are you alive?
React to the changes your body creates
Every curve moves from within need
Surpass the sensation to hold back and embrace all
Escape into the ideas of dramatic obsessions
X-rated is only the opinion, remember that –
You are the judge of your own femininity

This method of poetry was a style that Edgar Allan Poe wrote to the women he was obsessed with. There is a hidden message within the poem.

Love So Long

Oh' the abnormal feelings of missing her
More than expected and, of course, sadder
The trunk is filled, the boxes marked hers –
Are packed in her car and the engine has started
And as she pulls away she says – nothing
The sorrow is not the loss of her company –
It is the constant reminders of the little trinkets left behind –
A hairbrush with blonde strands mixed in the bristles,
Heart-shaped soaps somewhat
dissolved from evening candlelit baths –
Lost and forgotten musical recordings
and photographs of smiles –
But the one thing that will soon be missed is her scent
The nectarous vaginal perfume she surrounded my penis with
That primal driven fervor will be missed most of all
Nothing compared to the aroma of her remaining after sex
But within a week of showering her pheromone will fade
away –
Shared thoughts, old movies at two a.m. and the last time
She touched me and meant it will be missed
Will this love remain just a memory,
like all of the ones before her?
And these feelings of her just
become passing slowly fading thoughts?
It is final, the car has driven out of sight
down the poignant road
On the balcony where we danced I stand and brush my hair
With her forgotten worn out bristled hairbrush
Mating strands of her blonde hair with mine
Moments later tears finally fall and the
ability to smile is nowhere to be found
Looking down the road hoping
that she forgot something important
And must return for it because like me at this very moment
She cannot live another day without it
whatever it was she left behind

"We are all conceived in close prison; in our mothers' wombs, we are close prisoners all; when we are born, we are born but to the liberty of the house; prisoners still, though within larger walls; and then all our life is but a going out to the place of execution, to death."

John Donne

And I Wait

11:30 p.m.

Have you ever tasted the blood of someone who lies dying at your feet? I have. I can still picture the liquid pouring like a broken water pipe from the veins of women and, yes, even children. Oh', the way it would discharge into my mouth. Gulp after gulp I would drink, until I could not take in any more. At least for the day my teeth would be stained a lovely burgundy when I was finished, that's how they caught me. Metallic odors similar to well water would linger on my breath for hours. During those moments I would allow my tongue to dance along victims tender warm skin. Tasting their fear. This was the only way that orgasm could be reached: An orgasm beyond belief.

Nothing I'm saying here is news to the world. Every doctor, journalist and psychiatrist has interviewed me over the last ten years. Books, magazine articles and even a film and nothing in the world has changed. What did the 'Daily Post' call me "Hungry-Man Eddie?"

You will all enjoy the fact that the chain of my lineage stops at midnight. My hands shall in no way penetrate the bodies of women again. Never will I feel their smooth skin, the sticky texture of their intestines as they slide from their bellies like an angry snake across the floor. Nor will I be able to recall the color of their blood before the air touched it, changing it from dark purple to cherry red. And let's not forget the sounds of delicate bones bending and snapping like twigs. Never again will I feel so very much alive.

11:35 p.m.

And I wait covered in an undersized blue blanket on the cold cement floor. A plastic tray next to me holds empty dishes that not long ago held my last meal: Macaroni and cheese and a root beer. I stare in a meditative state at the long cement cracks on the floor that are filled with the tears from men who have sat before me. The guilty ghosts wait, in spirit with me inside a secure unit made of steel bars, three inches apart from one another, three and one eighth inches apart to be exact, spanning six feet wall to wall.

Children stop screaming long before the elderly do. Long over dramatized echoes come blabbering out of the elderly. Each time I was reminded of an out-of-tune soprano singer. The children, most of them anyway, behaved, like children are supposed to do. I think maybe when it's happening the elderly hang onto their dreams as the beating begins. They [the elderly] leave reality and go on a trip back to somewhere in their history, a thought and a mental phone call to their children. I am not sure why but they leave mentally long before I'm finished.

Children only have limited dreams. They have had only a short amount of years to dream them. The elderly had years and years of dreams, ideas, goals; wasted time - the time that was never spent the right way. Until I knocked on their door, snuck in through their windows and waited for them inside their closets as they went to follow a dream hoping it would come true.

I smell the electricity in the air. Testing again. Perfecting again. The primal cries that have been sung from the E chair hover all around the cellblock, singing to me on this special occasion.

My screams will never be sung. No one will hear me begging or pleading. I will never drop my head and wish for another chance at this false realism. My arms are open, and I welcome death. I wonder as I sit here on the cold cold ground what death will taste like. Probably not as good as the young. But then again it couldn't be any worse than an eighty-three year-old woman, the one who thought I was her son when I walked out of her closet holding a straight razor above my head. She looked into my empty eyes and said, "Robert did you bring my grandson?"

I reached out to her, hugging her, holding her, the life and the memories she had lived rushed into me. Then I shoved my tongue into her mouth. How much she had learned in her life. She knew how to respond to a kiss, an aggressive kiss. That woman knew a life I would never know - I sliced her throat with a 9" hunting knife and drank her blood, hoping against hope to taste her dreams.

There is something that the very young and the elderly relate to. The one thing that makes them the same: waiting. They both wait in limbo. One waits to die. The other waits to live. There is nothing more important than that, nothing more human than waiting. In between the years of the elderly and the young, I wait for death and at the same time I wait for life. I'm in the moments, which teeter back and forth between old age and childhood.

11:40 p.m.

Three seconds ago the twenty till midnight death bell sounded. I can still hear the faint clatter of the bell echo all around the yard. I hear the doors down the hall opening. My waiting is up. My dreaming is over. Nothing matters. Time is now! Sitting here all this time I have realized one thing: It's not the waiting that has worried me all my life, it's the moments in between that have. The moment I'm in right now - as I was yesterday, and every day since birth, that's what kills us all.

As soft footsteps draw closer to me, so do the fundamentals of freedom. I want to stand up and dance! Waltz, tango, fox trot all the way to the E chair. The idea of lifting up my legs and dancing down the hall makes me feel so alive! Everything about this place makes sense right now. In twenty minutes it might not, in twenty minutes it won't matter, in twenty-minutes I'll be liberated. Now I know why they all did it, the ones before me. It's a release from the wait, from the worry and fear during the moments before the walk down the hall. They were not fighting death. They were celebrating it!

11:50 p.m.

No, I won't dance down the hall to the room with the E chair. I'm going to save my energy. I'm going to save all of it up so I can hit that high note during my visit on the E chair. I'm going to sing, sing and sing until the wait is over and my dreams can finally come true. Dreams that I've saved inside of me since I was a child, dreams that never amounted to anything as an adult. Now I know why the men before have screamed as the volts of currents seared through their bodies. My God, it was not for remorse or fear of dying. No, it was the screams of joy! The wait is finally over and a new unlived world waits for me! Good Night, unmerciful world it's time for me to go. There is nothing more for me to say. I must go and get ready; my audience has gathered and they want to hear me sing my songs as I sit strapped to the E chair.

12:00 a.m.

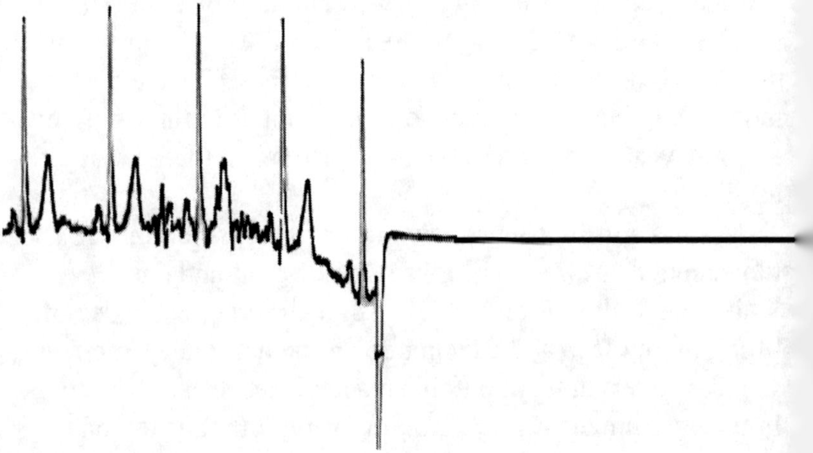

The Stranger Aboard My Brain

As the night dripped away to the sunrise
Moments of our hours past made us embrace closer
And we continued to dance while lying side by side
Zestfully our hearts mated like nature's feast
Every breath was another contour of devotion
Memories seared into our unconsciousness
Engulfing the physical space around us
"Are we just beginning our feel for affection?" You asked
"Never forget this gentle moment." I replied
Nothing can take away our obsession.'
Along with the waking sun we awoke to each other

ReLAX

And we sat side by side, surrounded by the meek
Not a friend around to damage our short time together
Nobody to gaze at us like we did with one another
Anna moved with sultry poise around my mind
Damning the demons within me to retreat
Only time will tell the damage we shall cause
Negotiating to the world for another encounter
Tuesday? Wednesday? It's all an illusion, I tell myself
Bring on the demons and let me wrestle them again
Romance has no chance of surviving, they tell me
Endless questions haunt me as she walks onto the plane
Are you as intoxicated as I am? I tell her but she does not hear
Kissing her soft lips reminded me of youth, behind the school
Marriage is the demon! There I said it and now what?
Yell at me if it helps you communicate, but never cry
Hearts never mend while tears are running the show
Endless words randomly comes to mind as she flies away
And yet every word is spoken and there is nothing to do
Release the demons to the world and live like the insane
Together we shall inherit the world

"Zen . . . does not confuse spirituality with thinking about God while one is peeling potatoes. Zen spirituality is just to peel the potatoes."

Alan Watts

Jizo

Dark clouds parted, clearing the rain from the street allowing the passengers inside the Toyota Camry to see the red traffic signal. Seconds after the car stopped a steel hammer shattered the driver's side window; glass flew inside of the car. The hammer clipped the driver's ear.

Know one inside realized what was happening until the first, second, third gunshot echoed the street. A hand reached in, unlocked the door and opened it. The driver, caught in the seatbelt could not react in time. The hand that opened the door pushed a semi-automatic 9mm into his chest and pulled the trigger. Before the recoil could catch up to the smoke of the gun another bullet was fired over the driver's head into the chest of the male passenger directly behind him. Another bullet was fired hitting the passenger in the back seat in the neck, exiting his ear, shattering the back window and lodging itself across the street into the wall of a Chinese restaurant.

During this commotion a young man in his early thirties sat in the front passenger seat and watched. Bullets and glass danced like fireflies in a hailstorm all around him. He observed the gunman reach into the inside front pocket of the driver, taking his wallet, then move toward the back seat when a siren in the distance was heard. The gunman took off running down the soaked street, a 9" hunting knife fell from his person and stray dog placed it in his mouth, loping behind.

The man in the passenger seat opened the door and stepped onto the dark, damp city street. This was not the best neighborhood to wait in, but it was the only route that had quick freeway access from the baseball game. He walked over to the curb, sat down and watched small particles of trash float down the gutter. The sirens grew louder. Red and blue flashing lights came closer. They got nearer from all directions, brighter, louder.

The man continued sitting on the curb as the

police marked the areas surrounding the car with yellow tape. He watched as the paramedics removed the bodies of three dead men from the vehicle. After the arrival of the police, firemen and paramedics arrived. The surrounding streets were cornered off. Men and women in uniform scrambled around the Toyota as the man sat unnoticed. He watched as the bodies were covered in white sheets that turned red from the blood.

After more than four hours the excitement of the crime calmed down. When the very last report that could be written was finished, the man on the curb stood up. He started walking down the street in the same direction the gunman went, away from the flashing lights and yellow Crime Scene tape.

TWO

The flashing lights of the police cars could still be seen as the man walked into the only lit building on the block. The sign on the door read "Introduction To Loss". Inside the office building an empty desk where a receptionist during the day most likely sat. The carpet matched the walls: 25 years of cigarette smoke yellow. Once, long ago they might have been white. One lonely plant that had not seen water since Nixon lay dead in a terra cotta pot. Three dead leaves of the plant rested on the two-seated green vinyl sofa, which was ripped at the corner of both arms and repaired with silver duct tape. Overhead blinking like a strobe light at a Halloween party a fluorescent ceiling fixture, powered by four seven foot bulbs, three of which have burned out, provided some light.

He sat on the sofa, tossing the leaves from the plant back into the pot. The age of the sofa at least made the sitting comfortable. Before he could even cross his legs and actually relax the door to his left opened and a man in a dirty three piece suit that had seen better days walked up to him, hand out and clipboard under his arm. The man leaned up from the vinyl sofa and started to stand up.

"Hello, young man. You must be Christopher." He

glanced at his clipboard "a Bloom, Christopher Bloom, correct?"

"Yeah… but how did you know that?"

"That's not important. You must be tired from all of the excitement. But there will be plenty of time to rest later. Now we must join the others." He pointed his hand to another door to the right of the sofa. "The class started five minutes ago. But no need to worry, you'll catch on." He walked towards the door and placed his hand around the knob, but before he opened the door he turned and faced Christopher Bloom.

"Mr. Bloom beyond this door it all happens. Your journey into a new career will begin. Everything you feel right now will no longer exist." The man moved his face closer to Christopher's. "Mr. Bloom… we really need more of your kind here. Thank you for coming so quickly." He turned the knob and Christopher grabbed the man's shoulder.

"Excuse me… where am I? Should I be here?" The man turned, smiled and opened the door.

"Everything will be explained, Mr. Bloom." The door swung wide open. Bright over-head lighting made Christopher wince. Twenty-two heads turned and looked as Christopher Bloom entered into the first day of his new life.

THREE

Stepping into the room the tiled floor of what looked like a classroom, twenty-one people turned back around and watched the man in front of the class point to chalk-written instructions on a blackboard.

It was somewhere between Christopher's second or third step that he collapsed to the floor. His mind became overwhelmed with intense feelings of fear, anxiety and depression. His breath labored and sweat formed across his brow.

"Can't breathe, can't breathe." he mumbled barely above a whisper. Holding his hands tightly against his stomach as chills ran up his spine into his scalp and down across his cheeks. His lips trembled and his eyes began watering up. Christopher looked up at the clipboard man and was overcome with sadness, thumps upon thumps of deep and excruciating sorrow. Tears ran uncontrollably down his face, dripping onto the floor.

"It will be all right, Mr. Bloom. Please follow me to your seat." The man held his hand out.

Words would not come out of his mouth. He tried telling the man that he was dying - crying - unable to think or feel anything but sorrow. He tried, but just bent down again - letting out a very loud sob, a roar that was centered deep within him.

"Oh' God! Make it stop! Please take these thoughts away! I, I can't breath. I can't -stop them please -"

The man bent down next to Christopher. "Christopher, these feelings, they are all you have. This is all you are. Please try and stand up. I know it's the farthest thing from your mind but you will feel better once you're up." Again the man held out his hand and this time Christopher grabbed onto it like a life preserver and stood up from the cold unforgiving floor. Slowly some clarity returned to him, but the feelings of sadness - deep levels of suffering did not leave; would never leave. He also noticed something else; the man's hand had no sensitivity. He was grasping it very tightly, but it felt like big puffy clouds that float low in the sky on spring days. And that is what he thought of, thick white beautiful clouds on a spring day. The touch reminded him of childhood and how he imagined what the clouds way up in the sky felt like; weightless pillows. That was the texture of the man's hand. It was also the way the man's shoulder felt as he rested on it as Christopher went to his seat.

FOUR

Just by looking at the wooden chair you would get the sensation of uncomfortable. Christopher placed his hands on the worn table in front of him, nothing but heavy clouds.

"Mr. Bloom, just sit here and try to catch up on the instructions. I will come back for you in a few hours." The man touched Christopher's shoulder (heavy clouds). "It's okay to cry, Mr. Bloom it's all part of the job."

Christopher did not look up at the man as the cloud left his shoulder. "Nothing" he thought to himself "I feel as if I am nowhere just a ghost." He glanced at the woman sitting next to him. Nervously she wrote on a notepad in front of her. Christopher watched her. Every time she jotted something down on her pad her delicate silver earrings jiggled. He looked at the gray in her hair just starting to show from the roots. She must be in her early forties. Very well put together. Her dress looked brand new or freshly ironed. Her neck was just starting to get light wrinkles. She had nice curved breasts, from what he could see from the profile view he had. Also her arms where - something was wrong - he was missing something.

Christopher looked at the woman more intensely. He watched her lips tighten together as she wrote, her earrings jiggle, her neck stretch to one side and her breasts heave as she breathed in and he noticed that also with the loss of touch he had no feelings, no sexual feelings of any kind. He moved slightly closer to her, to take her in. Nothing, he could not smell her perfume or even the cup of coffee in front of her. He looked around the room like a lost dog, sniffing the air around him. Nothing. His eyes darted back and forth around the table, the people, everyone taking notes. He picked up the pencil sitting in front of him and put it in his mouth. He bit down and chewed part of it. Nothing. The pencil had no taste, no touch, no smell.

The man in front of the room stopped writing on the board and stared at them. His eyes glanced over the crowd as his arms went behind his back, his fingers locked together.

"Everyone this is the most important item I can tell you today, so please listen up." He stepped back, unbuttoned his jacket and slipped it off. The gray jacket was placed on top of a chair near the front of the room. Two small sweat marks remained on his shirt, under his arms.

"Okay there are twenty-one - sorry, twenty-two of you here today." He looked at Christopher. "Hello, Mr. Bloom." He turned his attention back to the people sitting in the chairs in front of him. "There are twenty-two of you and after today only one of you will get the job."

Suddenly Christopher found it hard to breathe. His stomach tightened. Chills ran up his back. Cold beads of sweat formed on his brow. He pushed the chair back from the table and slipped to the floor. He could not hear what the man was saying to everyone. He tried looking up at them as they scribbled. Tears ran down his cheeks. Again he sobbed deep from within and collapsed.

FIVE

Christopher could not determine the time he spent on the floor. The severe anxiety attack still lingered. When he slowly grabbed the chair and sat back at the table he saw once again everyone copying what ever was being written on the chalkboard by the man up front. The feelings of fear and sadness still consumed him, but not enough for him to pay attention. The woman next to him still wrote. Christopher moved over to her to see what she was writing or what he was missing during the panic attack. Once more he was overcome with feelings of fear, yet something was different. The feelings were not as bad as they had been, but still heavy enough for him to try and catch his breath. Heavy enough for his palms to sweat.

It was more than panic, he thought. He still could not actually pinpoint the anxiety, nor could he make sense of it. Also he had a dire need to pay attention to this job, whatever it was. The rent was three weeks late and he had no money left in the bank to pay it. The phone had been turned off four days ago and his daughter, his little six year old was getting tired of eating rice and peanut butter everyday. The rent, this job, his daughter, the bills, the car insurance, groceries, shoes, medical insurance - on and on he was assaulted with these thoughts of less than; insecurity filled him. He was overcome with feelings of fat and old, unloved and broken hearted, but not his own.

The woman next to him slowly turned her head. She looked into his eyes and did a very miraculous thing: she smiled. As her lips slightly parted Christopher sensed the tears running down his cheeks. They rolled off his face and plopped rain on the desk. The woman turned back and flipped to a new page in her notebook.

Christopher's head swayed back and he allowed himself to engulf the feelings. The feelings were of the woman sitting next to him. It was not his rent that was unpaid, or his daughter who was hungry. The woman next to him was the one who was scared. He closed his eyes, took a deep breath stood up behind her and rested his head on her shoulder. He hugged her. He held onto her as she wrote that was coming out of the instructor's mouth. He held her and rocked his head back and forth as feelings of despair and fear surrounded every cell in his being. There was no other feeling inside him expect sadness. Sadness beyond human thought. A few moments later the door opened and the man with the clipboard walked in and asked Christopher to follow him into the next room.

SIX

The well-lit room was about the size of a large closet. An empty water cooler stood dusty in the corner. Christopher sat down in another wooden chair and starred at the nicotine stained windowless walls. He looked up and counted three fluorescent light bulbs, all of which worked. In front of him was an unadorned steel desk, rusted in many spots. On the desk he saw were arms had rubbed away from the steel, leaving a dull gray area. An office chair was pushed in behind it. Leaning back into the wooden chair, Christopher realized that the anxiety had lessened. This made breathing a bit more easier, not more comfortable, but a little easier none the less. The door behind him opened and he assumed it was the clipboard man.

"Hello Mr. Bloom." It was the same man.

Christopher followed the man as he closed the door and walked around the desk sitting in the old chair. The man tucked himself comfortably behind the desk, placing the clipboard on top of the desk and his arms in the areas of worn away.

"Do you have any questions, Mr. Bloom?"
Christopher pondered for a second, but before he could speak the man said "Actually, Mr. Bloom, it would be more comfortable for me if I called you by
your real name." Puzzled Christopher waited.
"Jizo, as I was saying do you have questions?"

His mind formed no questions as he looked at the man, then at the water cooler, then to the rust spots on the desk. His eyes began watering. His bottom lip trembled as tears ran down his face. Then he spoke, "I'm scared." He wiped the tears away from his cheeks. "I feel like I should have questions, millions of them, but my mind is blank. All of this," he pointed around the room "seems normal to me as if I had been here before and I'm so afraid, so terrified. I pause before each breath because I fear the next breath will bring the panic back and the more I breath the faster the feelings rush into me - I'm stuck in this cycle of fear and I can't slow down to understand it."
The man put up his hand up as a kind gesture that he had heard enough.

"Jizo - I have learned through the years that the easiest way for you to understand this is to just tell you quickly and then fill in more details as time goes on." Jizo took in a deep breath, wiped the last tear from his cheek and sat up straight.

"What was that classroom about?"

The man looked at his shoes, "We call it birth. Those who possess the capacity to experience another human beings suffering are born, here, were you sit." He took Jizo's hand. "The people in the other room are poor and uneducated. They are trying to make a better life by learning a new occupation."

"What about the woman?" Jizo said.

"She, my dear Jizo, got the job, somehow she released her uncertainties and found the courage to apply herself... thanks to you."

SEVEN

"At first it caught us by surprise you coming to us. But when we sat down and recalled the last moments of your life it made sense to us. It was astonishing to witness such an occurrence."

Jizo relaxed a bit in the chair, paying close attention to the man's words and forgetting his breathing.

"You see, Jizo, the person you were before you walked in here does not exist anymore. You have no conscious or subconscious recollection of that person, nor do I. Exactly nine hours ago, three blocks from here you died." The man paused looked up at him, saw no expression and continued. "There was a robbery inside a car that you were in. The automobile stopped at a traffic light and a man with a gun approached the automobile, opened the door and killed you and three other people inside."

"I'm dead? Is this heaven?" Jizo finally asked.

"Yes and no." The man sat back in his chair. "Jizo, my name is Arahant. I'm a Guards Man; some refer to me as a Guide or an Adviser. Use whatever you are comfortable with. You were not a Buddhist, were you?" Jizo looked confused. "No need to answer the answer is no." Arahant reached out. "Take my hand. This will probably be the only time you will ever feel anything beyond human suffering." Jizo put his hand in Arahant's soft palm, no sensation. "Jizo, you have a rare chance to witness your death along with your rebirth. I'm doing this for reasons that will be explained to you in a few moments. I have never done this for anyone before." Arahant gripped Jizo's hand and darkness filled the small room. Moments later Jizo could smell rain in the air, rain that had stopped falling moments ago but left a moist, sweet smell behind.

AWAKENING EIGHT

Arahant and Jizo stood on the damp streets of the city. Arahant held Jizo's hand as a mother would do her small child when crossing a street. They walked next to a man in a hooded sweatshirt who had just emerged out between two buildings. They followed him as he walked down the street.

In the distance on the desolate city street, under a clouded dark evening sky, a Toyota Camry stopped at a red traffic light. They followed the man as he crossed the street, walking toward the Toyota.

Jizo watched as the man reached behind his back and pulled out a hammer tucked beneath his sweatshirt. Inside the Toyota sat four men talking and laughing. Arahant led Jizo to the front of the automobile.

They watched as the hooded man raised the hammer over his head. The steel hammer swung down and as the window began break, Arahant raised his hand and the tragedy-to-come paused.

"Jizo, please observe these events very carefully. Time will continue at half its regular pace. It is important that you learn how you came to be with us." Jizo was silent; he gripped Arahant's hand tighter as he looked at himself sitting inside the Toyota, frozen in time. The laughter on Christopher Bloom's face was so very foreign. Not so much his face, but the feeling of laughter.

The surrounding world moved like an instant replay of a football game, in slow frame-by-frame motion. The glass of the window spidered and then slowly imploded all about the car. The head of the hammer grazed the driver's ear, splitting it open. The passengers slowly turned their heads as the hammer fell somewhere in the car and the hooded man unlocked the door. As the door swung open the hooded man reached into his pocket and removed a handgun.

"Watch closely." Arahant said as they walked around the Toyota to the passenger side.

The hooded man pushed the driver against the seat and placed the gun to his chest and pulled the trigger. Life from the driver floated about the car with the smoke of the gun and then faded. Jizo watched as Christopher tried unbuckling his seatbelt in a slow frantic manner. The two men in the back tried doing the same. Then another gunshot went off hitting the man in the seat behind the driver in the chest. His life also floated away with the smoke of the gunshot. Then Arahant raised his hand and time in its illusionary state froze again.

Arahant led Jizo to the rear of the car; they looked inside at the occupants frozen in time. "It's important that you observe what happens here" Once again time returned to the slow motion state of existence. In the front passenger seat Christopher had unbuckled his seatbelt, opened the Toyota's door as another gunshot went off. His foot had stepped on the damp street and Jizo was face to face with himself. He watched as the gunman pulled himself out of the Toyota and pointed the gun over the roof of the car, firing once at Christopher's head, missing him. Arahant moved out of the way as Christopher slowly ran past them. He was three feet from them when another shot was fired. Arahant stopped time just as a bullet was two inches behind the skull of Christopher Bloom.

Arahant led Jizo in front of his former self. He then walked around him getting eye level with the bullet. "Watch, Jizo, this is your fate - your welcoming." From the angle they stood Jizo could see the bullet and the back of Christopher's head. Arahant pointed over Christopher's shoulder. "What do you see ten feet in front of you, Jizo?"
Jizo peered over Christopher's shoulder.

"I see that restaurant" He remarked, pointing.

"Yes, a restaurant." They walked in front of Christopher again.

Arahant pointed at Christopher's eyes. "Look where he is running to." Jizo starred at Christopher's eyes, turned and followed the direction to the eating-place.

"Is he? Am I running for shelter?" Arahant smiled. It was the first time Jizo had ever seen an expression come from his face.

"No, look beyond the eatery." Arahant placed his hand on Christopher's chest. "These are your last thoughts." Time started back in motion again, but even slower than the previous state.

Every three seconds movement in the illusionary world moved forward. The bullet sped closer. Three seconds later it touched Christopher's hair. Three seconds later it pierced his scalp. Three seconds later it cracked the casing of his skull. Jizo took in a deep breath, his body tensed. He was feeling Christopher's thoughts. Panic consumed him; fear more intense than an actual gunshot filled his being. Three seconds later the bullet touched his brain. Jizo was not feeling Christopher anymore - he was Christopher. In the near motionless reality he could feel the burning of the bullet as it tickled the outer lining of his brain.

"What are you seeing, Jizo?" Arahant said.

Jizo watched with Christopher's eyes as he looked toward the Chinese restaurant and stared inside the window. Three seconds later the bullet entered the center part of his brain, splitting the right side from the left side with searing heat.

Jizo looked inside the Chinese restaurant at a flashing neon sign that read "Closed" and right next to the sign was a gold statue of the Buddha. A shade from the sign reflected in the statue. Three seconds later the bullet began to exit the frontal lobe of the brain. Jizo looked at the gold statue and captured the image of children hanging off of the Buddha as the Buddha sat smiling right into Christopher's eyes. Three seconds later the bullet protruded from Christopher's forehead. Jizo stared at the Buddha. He could see the statue's big round face smile at him as the bullet began to exit his skull. Three seconds later the bullet sat in front of Christopher's face. Jizo could hear an echo of Christopher's subconscious exclaim, "What a beautiful image; kids laughing, playing on top of their god." Three seconds later Jizo's feelings of Christopher went blank, the fear subsided and the bright lights of the small room filled his eyes.

NINE

Arahant let go of Jizo's hands. "Welcome, Jizo, welcome to your journey."

Jizo's eyes squinted as they adjusted to the bright light of the room.

"What am I?"

Leaning back Arahant said. "No, my friend. Since the beginning of its existence everything that dies, the core matter of humans, animals, all sentient beings everything enclosed upon the earth never leaves. When a human dies their core being some people call it a soul, science calls it matter returns to the last thought of their subconscious. If someone dies and they are thinking about their dog they had as a child, then in most cases they return as a dog. If they are looking at a rose, when they draw their last breath then they will return as a rose. Almost everyone has a last subconscious thought before they die. But you, Jizo, your last conscious thought was of the Buddha himself. More importantly it was of the purest human form, children laughing and playing upon the perfect human being. In that last subconscious thought smiled as you had begun to die. Forgetting your own suffering and awakening to the pure reason for life on earth: love and happiness. In that final moment, Jizo, you reached enlightenment. It's rare for someone to never have known the teachings of the Buddha to become enlightened. But it does happen, as you are proof to that. The transformation is called Pacceka. To be enlightened without knowledge." Arahant stood up from the chair, smiled, and then sat down on the edge of the desk.

"But more than being enlightened, Jizo, you went even

further. Some beings on the verge of liberation from the material world choose to stay back in order to help all other sentient beings liberate themselves from the eternal cycle of rebirth and suffering. They refuse to leave the material realm until all creatures are free. These compassionate Buddhas are known as Bodhisattvas." Arahant touched Jizo's knee. "And for this journey that you vowed to honor they have named, Jizo." Arahant smiled again. "Bodhisattvas have limited senses, as you might have noticed. You have no taste, no smell and no touch. Those illusions will hinder you from helping everyone. Also, you have no sexual desire, no physical attraction, nothing that will divert you. Even the life you once had; friends, family, job, your memory - do not exist."

Jizo stood up. "The fear?" He turned and looked at the dusty water cooler. "The fear that is attacking me - that is the suffering of the people? I'm here to help everyone become free from suffering?" Jizo turned to look at Arahant "How?" He twisted all the way around the room and Arahant was gone. The small room held no one but himself. Jizo stood in the empty room for a few moments then turned, opened the door and walked down the dimly lit hallway. He did not know why, but it felt like the right thing to do. He opened the main door to the building and stepped out into the awaiting world.

JOURNEY I — TEN

It was still nighttime as Jizo stepped out of the building and onto the sidewalk. The last of the police cars had just started driving away. He watched as a police officer pulled down the yellow tape, rolling it up into a ball and tossed it in the back seat of a patrol car. The city tow truck drove past pulling the bullet-ridden Toyota behind. He watched as it turned a corner and disappeared a few blocks away. He was unclear of where he was heading or who he was supposed to help. So he just started walking down the sidewalk, until the darkness faded from the rising sun coming up in front of him.

Every so often he would stop and look around the city, wondering who was going to jump out at him and beg him to be saved. But no one jumped. The city had started to come alive with the daily commuters. Traffic had begun to pick up on the streets. As cars drove past him so did the suffering of the occupants, carried from the wind as it passed. The feelings came in waves. It was beyond his control to avoid them. Jizo decided to get off the main street and walk around the residential neighborhood to his left. It seemed calm and quiet. Maybe he could alleviate some of the fear. Since he had been walking the anxiety had started back at a steadier pace. Nine times he had fallen to his knees and wept. Passersby seemed not to notice him. They just went about their lives.

The neighborhood was filled with green trees and white picket fences. This was the neighborhood of the American dream. Every other home had a tricycle or baseball on the lawn. He watched as dads got in their cars with the morning paper under their arms, a briefcase in one hand and a cup of coffee in the other. The wives waved goodbye from the porch and the children sat at the breakfast table eating their eggs and toast. What a wonderful place to live, Jizo thought. But he soon realized that even the perfect families suffered. He gathered this from the feelings of panic that nearly overwhelmed him. As he passed one home after another the feelings engulfed him, the burden of mortgages, college funds, infidelity, alcoholism, spousal abuse, gambling debts, shopping problems, loneliness - it was to much. Jizo was deep within the neighborhood when he finally collapsed.

ELEVEN

Bright afternoon sunlight woke Jizo up from a sound sleep on someone's front lawn. Screams of panic echoed throughout his body. He held onto his head and rocked back and forth over and over again until his stomach churned and he threw-up. He could not stand the feelings. They had become more intense than anything he had felt so far "How long has it been? Three hours, three years, three hundred years? When does it lessen, when do I help someone instead of feeling all of them?" Wiping his mouth.

His mind was still swirling as he stood up and walked off of the lawn and onto someone's porch. Slowly he sat down on the cement steps and took in deep breaths. His legs relaxed a bit as he placed his hands in his lap, closed his eyes and just sat there in a meditative state. It was the first time he allowed his mind to feel the sufferings attacking him, but he would not let them stay in his mind. No they had to go!

His body relaxed in a perfect lotus position; one leg tucked under the other, crossed tightly against his body. His back was perfectly straight, as one hand rested on top of the other in his lap. The beauty was in his face, though. Every time a sensation entered his mind his lips would form a smile and emptiness engulfed him. The slower his breathing became the more relaxed he felt. This gave him even more strength to release the thoughts from his mind. Jizo remained in this meditative state for many hours and in that time not a muscle on his body moved.

TWELVE

When his eyes opened to the high noon sun he could barely feel his breath. For the first time since his rebirth calm breathing had begun. It was when he stood up from the cement steps that the panic overcame him again.
He leaned against the wooden, bent over and took in deep breaths. The house in front of him was dimly lit. He heard a radio playing at a very low volume. Jizo slowly walked to the front window and peering in saw a woman in her mid-forties. She was curled up on a couch with a blanket wrapped around her, pouring herself a glass of wine. By the puffiness surrounding her eyes you could see the remains of many hours of tears. Jizo left the window and walked to the front door,

opened it and stepped in.

Despite the warm sunlit day outside, the interior of the house was cold. It had a tremendous feeling of loneliness about it. He shut the door behind him and walked through the entryway and entered the living room. He stepped hearing a familiar song playing from the stereo to his right, but could not make out what it was. The woman brushed a piece of curly brown hair away from her face and looked at Jizo. She did not seem surprised to see him.

"Would you like some wine?" she asked him and then gestured for him to sit in an old armchair in front of her.

"No, I don't think so, I mean I'm not sure I can." He could instantly feel her suffering. His breathing became heavy and dark clouds of grief loomed over him. He tried releasing the thoughts out of his mind, but they would not leave. So he accepted them and looked at the woman.

"He died last night. I was at the hospital with him when he died. I held his hand and told him it was okay to let go." She paused and sipped on her wine. Jizo leaned in closer to hear her better. "Frank was such a fighter. Even when they told him -" she looked up at the ceiling "three months ago that the cancer was terminal, he still fought it. At first he just tried ignoring it, not talking about it. Pretending the medication was just a vitamin that he needed. He didn't even want our daughter to know. But she did. Every time she would call from school she would ask me, 'Mom, what's wrong with dad? He seems very distant.' I would just tell her that her father wasn't feeling well and he just needed to take the medicine the doctor gave him. I felt so bad lying to her. But that's what Frank wanted at the time." She adjusted the blanket on her, tucking it up around her neck.

Jizo sat motionless, trying to pay close attention to the woman's voice and not the constant attacks of depression overwhelming him.

"When we found out that the cancer had spread all over his body and was starting to attack his brain…" Her voice trembled too much for her to talk. Fast streams of tears ran down her face. Jizo fell to the floor unable to breath - he was overcome with feelings of the woman; her husbands death, her mother's death, how will she survive without him, the loneliness she was feeling. Every emotion the woman had been building up for all of these years injected themselves into Jizo's mind. The woman sat up from the couch and put he feet on the floor.

"When it started attacking his brain, I called Lynn and told her that her daddy was dying and that she should come home as quickly as she could. It happened so fast, within hours after the phone call."

Jizo took in deep breaths, his hands trembled, and chills ran up his back and turned into cold beads of sweat all over his face.

"Frank was slipping away. I told him it was okay, just let go. I told him that Lynn knew and that it was okay. But he hung on. With whatever ounce of strength he had inside of him he held on, until Lynn appeared at the door. As soon as she held his hand, even before she started to cry, Frank looked at her, smiled and died."

Jizo wrapped his arms around the woman's legs and held her tightly. The curves of her legs felt like heavy clouds. He held her as tight as he could and in a crying voice said "It's wonderful that he did not die alone! No one should ever die alone. He held on because it wasn't that he wanted to die without his daughter or wife around him. He held on because he wanted to share his last breath with his family." Jizo sat up on the couch next to the woman, placed his arms around her many quiet moments.

He could feel his breathing start to return to normal as he kissed her lightly on the cheek as he stood up. The woman watched him walk out of the living room. She took off the blanket that was keeping her warm. She heard the front door open and then close. She picked up the telephone next to her and called her daughter to tell her about the wonderful things her father did for his family.

THIRTEEN

Jizo saw someone sitting on the lawn. As he stepped off the porch, he glanced through the front window, the woman picked up the telephone, smiling.

"Is this what the end of suffering means? The understanding of human behavior?" He walked up to Arahant, sitting on the lawn.

"Jizo," he said motioning to the ground. "Please sit down." He sat next to Arahant, who was in full lotus position. He saw a tiny daisy growing out of the bile he left on the lawn earlier.

"You see, beautiful things come out of unpleasant things. One cannot survive without the other." Arahant lightly touched petal of the daisy and it swayed back and forth. "Look at you, for example. Your consumption of suffering allows others to smile. Where there is bad there is good. Where there is cause there is affect." Arahant reached his hand out and lifted up Jizo's chin so he could gaze into his eyes.

"You, Jizo, chose to help the suffering during your own suffering. What better example of Bodhisattva could I show you?"

"Arahant, the fear, the breathing attacks - it's like dying over and over. I feel my heart ripping apart." He pointed to the house. "That woman in there, why did I choose to walk into her house? Why, when almost every house I walked by creates the same feelings, the same fears of doom and confusion?" He tucked his legs closer to his body, exhaled and closed his eyes.

"My friend you will never get used to suffering. But I see you have found the path to meditation. You have found the way to ending the sufferings of your mind. The way to Nirvana." Arahant smiled at him. "Why does the earth exist, Jizo? How did the stars appear?"

Jizo opened his eyes. "I don't know."

"Correct. They are the questions of unimportance. Your task is to help those who are suffering. You have vowed to save them all. It does not matter who they are or why they are suffering, because they are no different than you are. Jizo? Look at me. They are you - there is no place where they stop and you start. You are very much apart of them, as they you. The difference is that you understand the sensations and they cannot."

Jizo slowly nodded his head and tears began to fall from his eyes. "Go to where you are needed, go to where you would never be needed. One day your journey will tell you where you must go. Until then travel into the world and save them all." Arahant stood up. "Meditate, Jizo - the suffering is all an illusion." Arahant placed his hands together and bowed. "When your journey speaks to you I will return one last time. Be well my friend, be well." Jizo wiped the remaining tears from his eyes and when he opened them Arahant was gone and two daisies grew instead of one.

JOURNEY II FOURTEEN

Almost fifty years had passed since Jizo watched the daisies grow on the lawn. It was the last time that he had seen Arahant. Fifty years since he had first learned about the ways of human suffering. Over the course of all those years estimated he must have helped ten, twenty thousand people. The magical thing about it was that Jizo could recall every one of them as if he had just left them. No person in his mind was more tragic than the next. Each of them had their own course in life. How wonderful for him to engulf their spirit and help guide them along the way.

He placed a dirty mop in a bucket of cleanser and sat down on a brown folding chair. Being there was hard for him. For the last twenty years he had gone no where else. It was not the true journey that Arahant told him about, but he felt he was on the right path.

Between mopping the floors, cleaning up trash and dusting the fixtures Jizo frequently had attacks. They started in his hands, trembling. Then cold sweats, feeling of distress would erupt from the center of his heart. He would, he had no choice, fall to his knees, screaming. Trying to sit up and start a breathing meditation would take almost three minutes. When his breathing would slow down just for a second, he would take that opportunity to sit up, cross his legs under one another, close his eyes and breathe deeply. These attacks have happened every five minutes of his newly awakened life for the last five years. It seemed that as the years had gone by he could rely on meditation for relaxing him to a point of alleviating the attacks by a few seconds each time. He sat on the folding chair with his eyes closed, breathing deeply and rapid, repeating over and over again, almost to the point of hyperventilation.

Today for some reasons the attacks came to him as they did in the beginning: every thirty seconds and some times quicker. Heavy clouds of depression loomed over his head, dark-menacing levels of fear, chills, cold sweats and even moments of pure human hysteria plagued Jizo to the point of exhaustion. For all that he had accomplished so he thought, the years and hours of meditation, the talks with people and their sufferings, nothing was quite like today.

"What was going on?" he asked himself in between the attacks. One thing for sure he could not meditate this away. So he chose to lie on the freshly mopped floor of the New Hope Community Hospital, the place he had mopped and cleaned for more than twenty years.

J izo showed up at the hospital after many years of searching the world for the purpose of his journey. It wasn't that he had traveled far. Actually he had never left the city that he died in, the city that he awakened in.

For the entire fifty years of his journey Jizo roamed the city, helping everyone that he came upon. The most powerful realization that he knew was that he never met a person who did not need his help. Everyone that he met needed really only one thing: someone to share his or her fears with. Some were more self-centered and suffered deeper than others, but suffering, pain, fear had no real measure to it. All sufferings had equal intensity. Life did not grant someone a greater fear or an easier grief.

Even as the nurses and doctors scrambled to their duties, Jizo curled up on the floor, pulling at his hair, screaming, sounds that echoed all along the corridor. No one around him could hear it. Or maybe they could, but screams from a hospital were as common as the approaching siren of an ambulance.

Then the anxiety eased up, his breathing slowed down to a near normal level and Jizo, still unable to stand, starting crawling. Using the wall he slowly crawled down the hallway, at times getting to his knees, but the fear was so paralyzing that he had to take short breaks. Closing his eyes, pulling his knees to his chest, he finally reached a doorway. Inside the room were two beds. The first bed with its clean sheets and pillow sat empty, waiting for the next patient. Near the open window lay an elderly man, balding on top of his head with patches of gray and white hair on the sides. His face was wrinkled in a way that only many years from living on the streets could produce. His eyes were closed as tubes fed him from I.V. bottles.

Jizo reached the bed and gathered enough strength to sit at its end. The man did not move. Jizo made him self more comfortable on the bed, positioning himself next to the man's feet. He rested his face on top of the man's legs
"An ambulance brought him in a week ago." Jizo turned to face the nurse who had just entered the room. She carried a fresh I.V. bag.

He could feel slight grief from the woman. Her red hair pinned in the back, she was a slightly overweight woman in her mid-thirties. A wedding ring glistened against the sun coming in from the window. Jizo felt her busy work schedule, the children, making dinner for her husband, paying the bills, doing the laundry and taking a few Percodan during the day had kept her children away.

"The paramedics said they found him lying in a ditch about four miles from here. He has no name, no valuables, nothing." She unplugged the I.V. from the I.V. tube and connected the fresh one. "He was mumbling incoherently when they brought him in, then fell into a coma." She tossed the empty bag into the trashcan by the window. She looked out the window for a few seconds and then turned to leave.
"No one has come to see him?" Jizo asked as she walked by the bed.

"He had a dirty backpack and an old dog sitting next to him when they found him. We put out a notice, but nothing." Smiling she adjusted her wedding ring and looked at Jizo. He smiled back with his head resting back on the man's legs. Tears started running down his face without him knowing. She turned to walk out of the room, but stopped to speak.
"Jizo" He sat up "This is were your journey begins."
He sat up a little. "I don't understand?"

The nurse walked back into the room halfway between the doorway and the empty bed.

"Along time ago this man enlightened you."

Confused Jizo looked at her. "This man?"

She took a few steps closer. "Not him - his Karma was the cause. You exiting the car and running away was the effect. Looking into the eyes of the Buddha as you drew in your last breath was the result." She knelt down and placed her hand on his knee. "This man is just the vehicle of your journey. Look around Jizo, beyond this room. It's what being leaves behind that is important. Because what if left will help the suffering of hundreds for many years… Everything is connected." She stood up and walked to the doorway. "Jizo, remember all sentient being suffer and you have vowed to save them all."

FIFTEEN

Jizo sat with the man for a few hours, trying to take in the feelings around him. Nothing came. So he sat and meditated next to the old silent man and still felt nothing. The sun was shining brightly through the window, directly on the old man's face. Jizo had no feelings of hate or anger for the man that killed him over fifty years ago. It was not part of his nature. Maybe this is why he stood up and walked to the window to close the blind.

His hand reached toward the rod that brings the blind down and then he saw. He lowered the blind fast and hard, turned toward the man. "Your suffering is over, my friend everything is where it should be." He walked past the man and could hear the heart monitor machine start to beep; once, twice and then one loud constant heavy beep followed him out in the hall.

When he reached the hallway he was for the time being no longer afraid, no longer in constant terror of the surrounding world. He ran down the hallway towards the stairs. Down the six flights of stairs he sprinted, through the main lobby he ran, never losing momentum. Once outside the hospital he raced through the parking lot, across the main lawn and down a hill. When he reach the backside of the hospital the feelings slowly started to return. He tried picking up speed and out running them, but the faster he ran up the back hill the faster the clouds floated over his head. Within twenty yards of the back area of the hospital Jizo found it impossible to walk let alone run. So he chose to crawl along the back lawn. On his hands and knees he moved. Closing his eyes periodically in order to meditate, but always moving ahead. He finally reached the top part of the grassy hill and twenty feet away from him he saw enlightenment.

SIXTEEN

At the top of the lawn sat an old, tired and hungry border collie. She stared up six floors at the window of where her master had just died. Her ribs showed through her fur. "She must have been there since they brought him in." Jizo thought as he approached the dog. She glanced at him, looked up at the window one more, for the last time and then lay down. 'All sentient beings suffer.' Jizo recalled the nurse saying to him. As he reached the dog the feelings of loss and confusion rushed into him. He placed his head next to the dog's face and then rested. The collar around her neck had a tag, which read 'Sangha'. Both of them remained perfectly still. Jizo could not read the dog's mind, but he could feel her panic: Where to go? How to eat? Who to follow? Who to please?

They sat touching each other as the sun directly above them beat down. Jizo placed all of the dog's feelings inside of hi, allowing them to come into his mind and then leave. Over and over again the same feelings came to him. 'So much confusion' he thought. Then he heard a crowd of people behind him talking and laughing. He raised his head, looked over his shoulder and saw a courtyard with nurses and children laughing and playing. He sat up, keeping his hand on the dog; her fur felt like heavy clouds. After all the years, it was never something he was used to.

"The world suffers all around us and yet we still find time to kick a ball across a yard and swing on an old tire." He looked down at the dog "Suffering is not enough." And with that he stood up. "Happiness, Sangha, if we are not happy, we cannot share it with others." He began walking down the hill toward the courtyard where the laughter came from. Every so often as he grew closer to the courtyard he would look back and watch Sangha watch him.

SEVENTEEN

The fence surrounding the courtyard was unlocked. Jizo opened a steel gate and walked in. He was amazed at what he saw and more importantly what he felt: nothing. For the first time in fifty years Jizo had no feelings. All levels of panic, grief and suffering had disappeared. His mind was not consuming the suffering of anything or anyone around him. He sat himself down on a wooden bench a few feet from the gate and watched as children, mostly with baldheads ran around and kicked balls and slid down slides. He observed children in wheelchairs with I.V. tubes in their arms laughing and smiling at one another. It must have been someone's birthday, because a cake with candles in it sat on a table. A clown walked around, making balloon animals, parents mingled and talked to one another. Jizo watched all of this and felt nothing but happiness.

Walking toward him along a pathway that separated the swings from the slides was the redheaded nurse from the sixth floor. She carried a balloon animal shaped like an elephant. Jizo watched her walk closer to him and still felt nothing. She smiled as she passed the children on the swings and bent down and flicked a piece of grass off of a little girl's cheek. She peered over to Jizo and handed the balloon animal to the girl.

"Hello again" she said to Jizo as she approached. Jizo nodded as she sat down next to him. A little boy with more hair then the rest of the kids came over to the nurse.

"Nurse Chambers, did you see the cake?" The boy was moving side-to-side, smiling anxiously.

"I did Tommy - how wonderful for you." The little boy smiled and ran off.

Before Jizo could ask the nurse explained to him. "You see Tommy? He's been in remission for one year." She looked over at Jizo and took his hand. "His fight is not necessarily over, but he has a chance to get stronger and if it returns the strength will be there to fight." She placed her other hand on top of his. "Heavy clouds, huh?"

Jizo moved his glance from Tommy and looked at the nurse. He was about to speak, but held himself back. Instead he cried. Slow droplets fell from his eyes.

"Children don't suffer like us?" He finally said.

She gripped his hand tighter. "Every sentient being suffers. But some," she pointed to the children and placed her hand back on his, "learn how to accept, then overcome their suffering. Children learn to accept the cause of their lives and can live in peace throughout the effects. It is when they grow up and take on the attachments of the world - mortgages, taxes, marriage, children - their own mortality, that they forget what childhood is all about - simplicity."

Jizo moved his hands away from her and wiped the dripping tears away.

"So children accept their suffering, their death and move on towards celebration?"

She gripped his hand tighter and said, "Until they learn different."

Jizo stood up from the bench and looked at the children laughing. He watched as Tommy blew out the candle on his cake. Jizo's eyes moved all along the courtyard from the swings, to the slide then to the black gate where Sangha now sat watching the children. Jizo looked at the nurse and said, "How wonderful!" then fainted.

EIGHTEEN

When Jizo woke up in the courtyard, on the wooden bench. The children were still playing, eating cake and Sangha lay outside of the courtyard on the grass, watching. The nurse stood over Jizo wiping his forehead with a wet towel. Suddenly he realized that he could feel the towel on his forehead. A hand that was holding his, that he could feel! The warm sensation of the nurse's skin touching his hand was unbelievable. He sat up, touched her face very slowly and felt her warm soft skin.

"Are you okay? You fainted a few minutes ago."

Jizo kept his hand on her face and marveled at the smells of flowers, trees and children all around him. "Did you bump your head or anything?"

Jizo stood up and took both of her hands into his and rubbed them slowly against his face. "Are you still dizzy? Do you need to lie down again?"

Jizo wrapped his arms around the woman and felt her body against his. The feelings of warmth and sensation of human contact were brilliant. He hugged her tighter. "Are you okay?" She asked with her head against his shoulder.

Jizo let go of the nurse, stepped back and nodded to her. He looked up at the sky, took in a deep breath and exclaimed, "I feel awake!"

He walked slowly around feeling each step on the ground. His mind was clear, alert and perfect. Every known suffering in life was within him, as were their causes and conditions. While watching the children accept their suffering Jizo had awakened to a place that can only be described as human understanding. The true connection that Jizo realized could never be explained in words. Words could barely describe the event. It is like a menu at a restaurant. The menu was just a description of the food, not the real food. The real food, the real feelings have to be experienced in order to understand them. But somewhere between the children and watching Sangha lay on the grass Jizo understood all of human suffering.

When he opened the gate, feeling the cold steel in his hands a profound thought came to him. He smiled and reached down to touch Sangha. The dog sat up and licked Jizo's hand as he touched her fur. The texture of the dog's fur was soothing.

"How wonderful you feel" Jizo said. He wrapped his arms around the dog. Over the dog's shoulder, sitting in the grass a few yards away in perfect lotus position was Arahant. He sat still with his eyes closed. Jizo looked at the nurse.

"Come on Sangha, let's take you home." The dog followed Jizo to the gate.

"This is Sangha," Jizo touched the dog one more time. "He needs love." The nurse reached down and petted the dog's fur and opened the gate to let him in. The dog trotted around inside the courtyard, smelling everything in front of him and then walked up to the children.

"How long have you been here?" Jizo asked her.

"I've been here for three hundred years."

"What about the feelings I felt for you?"

"Not me, but a manifestation of what this body represents." She took his hand and held it tightly. "Jizo, you are a great Bodhisattva, we have been waiting for you for a longtime." She took his hand and pointed to Arahant. "Your journey awaits you."

Jizo watched her close the gate and as he turned to walk away, he heard children laughing and playing with the dog.

"What will we call him?"

"He needs a bath."

"Is he hungry?"

"Do dog's eat cake?" The voices faded as he walked up the soft grass towards Arahant.

NINETEEN

Arahant opened his eyes and pointed at the ground. "Please, sit." Jizo sat, placing his legs under each other, taking in a deep breath of fresh air and relaxed his body into a lotus position.

"Jizo, awakened with the sufferings of the world." Arahant smiled.

"Arahant, this existence of mine I feel there is more for me."

Arahant stretched his legs out and reclined on his back against the grass. He stared up at the sky and observed a cloud floating overhead, "You are perfect Jizo - everyone you meet with, talk with or acknowledge will attain perfection - the suffering of the world will be over within a few hundred years." Jizo stretched his legs out and dug his hands deep within the green, moist grass. He loved the way it felt between his fingers. He just allowed the feelings of the grass to consume him.

"No, there is something more important I must do." Jizo finally said.

Arahant sat up and touched Jizo's knee. "What could be more important than helping the suffering world? Jizo you have attained perfection and the movement of your journey is all around -" Jizo placed his hand in front of Arahant; interrupting him.

He placed his hand deeper in the grass and could feel the dirt from which it grew on the tips of his fingers. "I must go to the place of pure human suffering." The feelings of wet dirt and cool grass slowly started to fade. "Beyond this realm of suffering there is a far greater land that needs me." The way the grass felt had turned into a feeling of heavy clouds. The texture, the temperature and the way the wind felt against his face, he did not even take in one deep last breath, he decided to let someone else enjoy it.

"My journey, the place I vow never to leave until all sentient beings are relieved of suffering is…"

The feelings of heavy clouds had returned, as did deep stages of fear, grief and panic far beyond anything he had experienced up to this point. But before the tears came and the lack of breathing consumed him Jizo whispered. Arahant placed one hand on the ground and the other in the air and smiled. The spot upon which Jizo sat slowly faded. His mind was assaulted with five billion emotions all-relating to suffering. He faded into dust before Arahant's eyes. When the dust around him finally settled a small perfect daisy grew where Jizo sat. A few moments later another daisy appeared, then another.

"He's saving them all." Arahant stood and started

walking up the grass hill toward the sun. He smiled as flowers grew all around him. As far as his eyes could see.

It was the last few words that Jizo spoke to Arahant that made the flowers appear. "My journey, the place I vow never to leave until all beings are relieved of suffering is hell."

Afterward:

Bodhisattvas:
Some enlightened beings, on the verge of liberation (nirvana) from the material world, choose to stay back to help all other creatures liberate themselves from the eternal cycle of rebirth and suffering. They refuse to leave the material realm until all creatures are free. These compassionate Buddhas are known as Bodhisattvas.

Bodhisattvas have many hands so that they can help many beings. From their tears, shed after hearing the lamentations of suffering souls, rises Tara, the goddess of wisdom. The compassionate Bodhisattva, with the aid of the wise Tara, seeks to alleviate all suffering.

The concept of Bodhisattvas comes from Mahayana Buddhism and is especially popular in East Asia. In Tibet, the most famous Bodhisattva is known as Avatilokeshvara. In China and Japan, the most famous Bodhisattva worshipped by Buddhists has a female form. She is known as Kwan-yin or Guannin.

Jizo:
Was the Bodhisattva who asked to go to Hell in order to save all those who suffer. He vowed to return only when all beings there have been released from suffering.

hai·ku (hì'k¡) *noun*
plural *haiku* also *hai·kus*

1. A Japanese lyric verse form having three unrhymed lines of five, seven, and five syllables, traditionally invoking an aspect of nature or the seasons. (Sex is nature)

To S_____
Across her belly
Lays my warm semen remains
Her hand rubs it in

To L_____
Nothing from her voice
Talking to me all alone
Only sex will speak

To A____
Leaning against me
Drips beads of her smooth warm sweat
My mouth can taste salt

To F______
Do you miss the rain
Grey clouds of mornings cold drops
Against your belly

To L_____
Breasts large, nipples brown
Eyes very sad and moving
A Botticelli

Give Them Enough Rope

The town discussed the storm, inside the badly maintained church. The thunder rumbled, bibles opened, pages turned but nothing from King James could stop the terror. Thousands of rope vines rained down. Rope like the Gallo's used; knotted with thirteen slips wrapped tightly in nooses with people attached. Their bodies swung ten feet off the ground. Crack, they echoed! The town hid under pews waiting for the storm to pass. "God is tossing back the unworthy!" Someone yelled. Moments' later figures of Hell appeared to collect their dead and left when the last churchgoers closed their bibles and stopped praying.

(Flash Fiction - 100 word Short Story)

"The pest, in a sense, is a very superior being to us: he knows where to find us and how-usually in the bath or in sexual intercourse or asleep."

Charles Bukowski

Welcome To The Feeding

Present

"For the life of me I cannot remember the darkness as it used to be. Even with my eyes closed the light colored sparkles bouncing across my eyelids wont turn off. It seems the more I concentrate on them, the brighter they become."

"So why not open them?" It was her voice that frightened me the most. Deep within her lives a hungry pack of wolves, which have not eaten a good meal in some time.

Being sexually gobbled by a carnivorous woman who smells fear dripping from your brow has become my existence and not by choice, but rather by means of prison.

"Because when I open my eyes the world returns and the bright lights poison my retinas and the smell... I cannot take the smell."

"We cannot live outside of what we do not know," her pause opened my eyes.

"This, right now is all we have. This is who we are. This is what we have become." She wiped the blood from her chin with the sperm-stained sheet. I just lay there, like a panicky infant. This life with her was too much for me. After catching my breath from the intense orgasm, my cock slowly softened to that of a wet noodle. I closed my eyes one more time and pretended it was a hallucination. Or better yet pretend that it never happened. But like always or at least like it has been for the past three weeks, this was who I became - a frightened man.

Across her olive skin reflected blood stains against the glow of the nightstand lamp. Did it affect her? I doubted it. Her feelings dried up long ago. Probably with cum of all of those who came before me. No, she was stronger than me. She's more certain of what is left for us. Her sweet soft hand touched my knee as her other one placed a cigarette in my mouth. I could smell the blood on her - it reminded me of the smell a bitch has when it goes into heat: the smell of hunger. She lit my smoke and got up from the bed.

"What a freaking mess." She said, grabbing a blood soaked towel from the floor.

She placed her lit cigarette on top of the dresser. Somewhere in the back of my mind I hoped it would fall, burning and engulfing us ...nothing. I closed my eyes again and tried to forgot.

“I’m full,” she said “Are you ready to go?” She asked.

Six Hours Prior

We sat outside. She was in a lawn chair that had seen to many Summers at the beach snuggling up to a pit of fire as Bob Marley jammed from a beat up portable CD player. I laid on the tree shaded cement, quite possibly the only cool area in the city. We pondered in our driveway, planning what the hell to do on this hot summer night in July. It was the usual banter of nothing certain.

"Maybe we could go to a movie?"

"No."

"How about a strip club?" The beauty of her blue eyes glanced at me. For a second I had Nietzsche's worst enemy in my mind... 'Hope'.

"I don't think so."

"Well when you find something you want to do, let me know." She lit another cigarette, dropped the pack by my foot, leaned back in the beach chair and opened her well read copy of Harry Shannon’s *‘Bad Seed’*. The creaking sound of the chair bothered me. I knew at any second that it was going to break. She tempted the chair, leaning back farther into it... nothing.

"Take me inside and fuck me." Direct requests from her are very sexy, but I was not in a sexual mood, which is quite unusual and would soon pass.

"It's too hot to fuck."

"Come on take me inside and lay me down in front of the fridge." Tempting, but I was missing something.
I looked down at her feet, the way her toes lined up in perfect

order, one not bigger than the next. Red polish painted across her nails, her anklebone flexing, as she rocked back and forth in the suicide chair... nothing.

"Come on take me inside. We'll watch some porn and I'll tell you about the girl at the gym who who's burning for me." She got me going on that one. "She's about five foot six, nice long brown hair, curly like mine and her breasts. Oh' her breasts are so sexy. She has to be a full C cup. Well my hands fit into them perfectly." She was baiting me. I looked up at her and tried not to give in.

"Hmm, so did you fuck her already?" I asked.

The smoke exhaled from behind her lips. She flicked the cigarette into the street. We both watched it die against the hot black tar rolling into the gutter extinguishing into fresh sprinkler water.

"No, but you would love her. She's a perfect weekend for us."

I gave in. "Well call her up."

"No, not yet, I'm still playing with her."

"Well you felt her up, how much more playing is there?" She waited for the car to pass before she said anything. It was our neighbors from across the street, a large Mexican family who must have all of their relatives from the old country living in a cramped three bedroom. The mother and her sister got out of the Dodge family van. We watched as the side door of the van slid open and two daughters got out. They looked at us and waved. We waved back.

"I touched her breasts when we were showering after our work out. She has implants and I asked her how they felt." She finally said. "I need some water, you want anything?"

"No." I replied.

Nina got up from the suicide beach chair, walked across our driveway, opened the gate and disappeared into the house. I sat on the cement lit my last cigarette from the pack of Camel Lights and stared at the oldest daughter of the two daughters, whose name escaped me. I watched as she bent down to talk with her younger sister and then followed her with my eyes as she walked into her house. The younger daughter walked across the street toward me. She would come over at times when we bring groceries home and help us with them.

"Hey you." I said because I also do not remember her name.

"Hi John... what are you doing?"

"Staying cool on the driveway. What are you up to?"

"Um nothing" She spoke with a slight accent; more street lingo than from Mexico, so nothing came out sounding like 'nuting'.

"Um Laura thinks you're cute."

"Hmm, who's Laura?" I figured it was her sister, but wanted to be sure.

"She's my sister."

"Really?"

"Yes, she watched you when you cut the grass from her bedroom window."

"How old is Laura?"

"She's... um... twenty."

I heard the gate open behind me. "Well tell her I think she's cute also."

"Okay ...Hi Nina." She waved as she darted back across the street, not looking for oncoming traffic and ran into her house.

"What did little Elizabeth want?"

My turn. "Her sister thinks I'm cute." I didn't look up at her, the chair creaked and stopped.

"You want to fuck her sweet Mexican cunt, don't you?" I didn't say anything. I figured it was a no win situation. I could say yes and she'd use it against me when she leaves me home alone. I could say no and she'd know I was lying and will use it against me when I'm fucking her for the simple reason that she would think I'm imagining Laura instead.

"Don't you?"

I pulled a cigarette from the pack and laid down on the still shady, very hard and uncomfortable cement. "I want to watch you fuck her." Exhaling my smoke.

Nina smiled at me and said "Well, I would rather watch you lay her on our bed and slowly kiss her brown skin. I want to see you kiss her toes, lick her ankle and slither your tongue up to her knee, across her thigh, biting it slowly. Then I want to see you spread her lips apart and suck her young wet clit. I want to watch her tighten her stomach, holding in her orgasm for fear of being so inexperienced with someone she hardly knows."

Reaching for the cigarettes she went on. I sat there with my eyes closed against the cement. I could feel my penis move as the thought raced into my mind, but something held me back from fully appreciating the fantasy - Nina. She has powers that destroy the things that she does not need. I could picture her during this scenario, getting into it, playing with herself as she hides in the room and watches me fuck our pure probably virgin neighbor.

She would watch until... "That's what we are going to do tonight!"

I finally opened my eyes and looked up at her. God, she is beautiful. Not in the usual way women present themselves. Nina had an eminence that was so powerful it scared me at times. A command that could asphyxiate anyone who tried going against her. A power that I felt she had when we first met 3 years ago. Even though at the time she refused to acknowledge from within herself, until it was all that was left for her to explore.

"Fuck her for me, John. Rape her cunt until it bleeds." God she could wake you up. She could love you and slice your heart open with one small kiss. I closed my eyes and beyond my control my cock went hard and it was all over, the Mexican nineteen year old would feel me soon and Nina would watch us until it was time for her... not to.

5 Hours Prior

I watched as Nina dressed. A purple towel laid around

her feet as she stood tying her white silk bathrobe. Her breasts dripped fresh shower water and she watched me watch her from the mirror's reflection. Her straight white teeth smiled at me. I stood up from the toilet, lifted the lid and tossed my finished cigarette into it. I didn't flush, the noise drives me crazy.

"I'll be ready in five minutes, why don't you go outside and see what happens." I stood up from the toilet, flushed it despite the noise and walked out of the bathroom, down the hall into the kitchen and out the front door.

As much as I was I wanted to taste and fill Laura I was hesitant. I have been down this road with Nina before. It never ends well... there is always a trail she leaves behind.

Welcome To The Feeding

I stood with a towel wrapped around me as I filled our juicer with mango, papaya, apples and carrots. Nina sat in her white silk robe looking at the wasps buzz around their hive through our window. We tried getting rid of them once but they came back and built a bigger hive, so we left them alone, as they did us. The slow grind of the juicer and the smell of the fresh juice always made the mornings calm. Over the sound of the machine I heard our front gate close. Nina stood up, fastened her robe tighter and opened the front door. Our visitor stood in the doorway.

"Good Morning, Laura," Nina's soft voice said. I had never actually talked with our neighbor. We always did the usual quick hello from across the street and that was the extent of it. But Laura was something Nina had been planning for a few weeks now. It was not a fluke that she was here. "Hi John." Laura walked into the doorway and stood just in a perfect way as the sun reflected her brown hair from the window.

"Good morning, Laura. How are you?" I asked as I walked over to Nina and handed her a glass of fresh breakfast juice.

"Would you like one?" I asked the neighbor.

"Yes, it smells great." She smiled and pure very sexy round full lips pursed. She walked over to the kitchen table and sat down. She was wearing a small black mini-skirt that rose very close to her sex as she sat down, man's white cotton dress shirt that was buttoned down to her cleavage. Her hair was almost like Nina's but longer with a bit more brown. Her feet sat inside a pair of opened-toed black leather shoes, like a sandal with heals. She stood about five foot four without the shoes.

Nine reached out and touched Laura's hand. She gripped it tightly, almost stopping the circulation. Their eyes locked like cats ready to pounce.

"Tell him what you want." Nina told her.

Without hesitation Laura "I've never been in your house before. It looks a lot like ours." Nina looked at me and smiled. I guessed that our meditation and our sexual practice was our secret. And I also guessed that Laura how no clue that she would be meditating with us in about ten minutes.

"Perfect juice, honey."

I let them talk as I cleaned the juicer and fed the cats. More than anything else I was excited by our morning meditation, especially adding a third person. We have talked it for a few weeks, but Nina wanted this, actually I think she needed this. Her sexual hunger had been growing and the level of our intercourse had taken a very powerful turn. The ability to sit with someone you love and cherish for hours at a time and the only way of communication is by touching, created another world for us. Nina's level of relaxation was a power to behold. Over the last year she has learned to control her vaginal muscles to the point of sucking my cock with them. It feels like nothing that I could explain with proper justice. She also had relaxed her body enough to allow her G spot to ejaculate cum during our sessions. But her real turn on, the thing that gets her to a higher level of passion was...

"Honey? Honey?"

Snapping out of my dream state I looked across the

room. "Yeah."

Nina looked at me smiling. "Did I wake you? You looked very far away."

"No, I was just thinking of a poem."

"Laura would like to meditate with us."

Our Guest

I finished the dishes and went into the spare bedroom that we had converted to our meditation room, or as Nina called it 'The Chamber'. The showers in both bathrooms were running. I heated up the oils in a baby bottle warmer. Nina made her own meditation oil from eucalyptus, ginger, spearmint and a natural oil base. The smell was wonderful from it, it never seemed to be too greasy and it lasted a long time before it evaporated into the skin. I turned on the compact disc player and switched Mozart for Debussy. The showers stopped almost at the same time. I lowered the blinds and blocked out all sunlight with the thick black curtain that we use on bright mornings like this.

The incense burned from two bowls at two different corners of the room. I chose to light jasmine and sage. I placed the velvet padded round pillows next to each other forming a circular triangle in the middle of the room. At this time Nina walked in still wearing her silk robe and Laura stood behind her in a similar robe.

"It smells wonderful in hear." Laura said looking over Nina's shoulder.

"Please both of you come in, I'm going to shower real quick. Walk around and take in the music and the incense." As I walked past them both Nina's hand touched me, her fingernail sliced my arm. As I turned around she walked into the room.

The morning shower is the best one. A good night shower is pleasant but not as powerful as one in the morning. I soaped myself up and rinsed off. My mind was working beyond the meditation and that bothered me. The soap ran from my body as I knelt to the shower floor and took in some deep breaths.

Laura's First and Last Time

By the time I got into the meditation room Nina and Laura had begun to meditate. They still had their robes on and seemed very relaxed. I walked past Nina and touched her hair softly and then I sat in front of Laura and watched her eyes move around behind her eyes.

"Laura?" I spoke softly.

She opened her beautiful brown eyes and looked at me inquisitively.

"Laura, have you ever meditated before?" She sat still and shook her head. Nina sat in perfect Lotus and did not hear or acknowledge us. Nina never explained what we do or what kind of meditation takes place. But I felt that she knew Laura would find this to be wonderful or Nina would not have asked her to join us.

"Well, this is Tantric meditation. We close our eyes and breathe to the thoughts of nothing. It sounds easy and well it is, but the breathing is what is important here. During the meditation you will, how should I put this, you will become very relaxed, maybe scared, maybe angry, maybe calm, but do not feed into any of your emotions. Let your mind feel the pain or joy and let it pass. As you pass from those feelings you will be elevated to a place outside the human consciences.

A place that only dreams can take you. It is at this moment that you can become alive."

"It sounds wonderful," she said almost in a whisper.

"It's more than wonderful it's rapture." She smiled.

I took her hand "The way of Tantric is our breathing will all become in sync. One will breathe out as another breathes in. If a hand touches you allow it to experience your skin, acknowledge it and move above the reaction, as your hands move around be aware of what they touch and move beyond it. Do you feel comfortable?" I could see her nipples become erect through the robe.

"It sounds nice." And she closed her eyes.

I stood up and lit three more candles and another incense. I hit the replay button on the compact disc player. I watched them medicate for a few moments. I saw Nina's breathing become slower and her eyes dance almost in a R.E.M state. I took off the towel from around my waist and dropped it on the floor. I knelt down in front of Nina and untied her robe. Slowly I loosened the belt around her and slipped the silk down around her waist. I moved over to Laura and did the same. Her eyes also waltzed inside of her lids and I dropped the silk robe around her waist and touched her hair softly. I sat Lotus with my back connecting to both of them and closed my eyes for what seemed like years, until I felt a pair of hands touch my shoulder and another pair touch my chest.

As I turned slowly around, I could hear the violin solo of DeBussy's "Delibes" filling the room along with the smell of jasmine. My head rested in Laura's lap. I could smell the warm meditation oil on her legs. Nina's finger ran down my back and her nails dug into my skin as she pulled towards her. My breath was alive, my senses open to everything. Laura's hand pulled my face towards her lips. I kissed her softly and gently. I could feel my cock touch the back of Nina's throat and as I opened my eyes I saw two beautiful women touching each other. My mind would not come back to me; it danced emotions I have never known up to that point.

I watched Nina spread Laura's legs apart, she poured oil on her glistening soft pink sex and then began kissing it. I turned around and did the same to Nina. I ate her sex and felt her cum down my chin. She stood up and knelt over Laura and ejaculated on top of her chest. Laura's beautiful full breasts dripped cum down to her belly. I kissed her thighs and watched her lick Nina's sex. Nina reached over toward me and guided my cock into Laura's warm wet cunt. I moved in and out of her with the same rhythm of Nina on top of her face. I watched as Nina grabbed Laura's breasts and rubbed them, bit them until they bled... Laura came all over my cock.

I slid out of her and moved over to the box that houses Nina's special toys. I pulled out a penis whip that Nina uses on her clitoris, a very well charged up cordless vibrator, two cold steel Keigal stimulators and a 9" hunting knife.

When I turned around Laura was on top of Nina, her teeth gnawing on Laura's brown nipples. Laura rolled off of Nina near unconsciousness, the blood from her nipples puddled between Nina's breasts. Nina rubbed it in and got to her knees and looked at me. I handed her the knife. Nina rolled Laura onto her stomach and began teasing Laura with the knife. With her legs spread apart she placed it lightly on Laura's ass. I knelt in front of Laura and rubbed her back, as she tasted me. Nina took her tongue and slowly licked along Laura's ass, teasing her cunt. Spit rolled down between her legs. Nina poured oil on her hands and body and them slowly placed one, two, three and four... her fingers inside of Laura. Cum trickled down, Nina bent over licking it and then fucked her faster. I pulled my cock from her mouth and looked into her eyes... she was not on Earth. Nina with her hand still inside of Laura, still fucking fast and hard laid next to her. I moved out of their way and watched. How insignificant a man is at some moments. It neither puzzled or bothered me. The joy of watching their pleasure was a comfort I enjoyed. Before I left the room and allowed them more privacy I brushed Nina's hair out of her face and whispered to her -

"It's time to move."

Nina smiled and said, "Go pack, as I finish up."

I closed the door and left them to take pleasure in each other. Let Nina devour her and pleasure herself on Laura's carcass. It was always the same, no matter what city we ended up in, Nina would feed her desire, until the prey ran out.

Oedipus Doula

Can it be the lies of humanity that drives man farther
into the sovereignty of mourning?
Men hold near and dear the bleeding of their
lifeless hearts for what reason?

Punishment is the secret quest of the
possessions that they cannot obtain,
Be it by supremacy, prosperity, intelligence, or charisma
Man suffers for one reason and one reason
only and that is to electrify, undress,
And suck the juice that drips from the cunt that
reminds them of mother's flavor
To drive the force of cock back into the woman of worship is
The only power a man thinks he has
Even it is to be a passing whore whose goal
is to give themselves for a chance at freedom
The accolades and contributions given along
the way of are nothing compared to the
Smell of perfume wafting from a woman's neckline
Bitter and betrayal sink man's teeth in
her nipples bleeding them
Till they drip mother's milk

Mother taught us without words to live for her,
die for her and to always love her
Madness taught us to hide in order to sustain
deeply from carnal pleasures
Without that all we as men are just executioners
who hunt down the things we live for
By means of rape and wounds, bruises and verbal assault

The very core of the woman that we so desperately
Need to get back into is our sorrowful fear

Never replace love with desire; it will just reject you
Remember love was lost when we escaped from
That dark pungent womb mother built for us

The journey began when we drew our first stench of breath
When we where flung out into the world to
        find the womb again
And when the time came for us to show our
        rewards to the Queen
All she, mother, could say was NO she is not the one,
        keep looking
The cunt who deserves my son waits for you,
        smell her out, and then come back
Until then close your eyes and sleep back inside me,
        rest there and once again be
My little baby boy who needs nothing more
        than what I can provide for you
Remember I am the source of your being and
Nobody can ever take that away from us even when they try

"It is the confession, not the priest, that gives us absolution."
Oscar Wilde

A Warm, Dry Place

I: Peer Of The Realm

There is a mile square area in the meat packing district of New York City that is not on any tourist map. This area has no postal route and as far as the police are concerned they only go there when they need to find Jimmy Hoffa. This area is known as Peer Of The Realm, named for its unholy host of peculiar and dreadful residents. If you live in the city, you refer to it as Peers. During the day Peers is a vampire, the streets, sleep waiting for the moon to open the coffin lid.

Snow has started to melt away from the overflowing trash cans lining the sidewalks. The scent of winter slowly fades from the stench of the late night buses whose exhaust choke the dead and dieing bums sleeping under cardboard blankets. Across each and every street beat-up prostitutes wrapped in faux fur walk along the corners, looking for various ways to trade their souls to john to maintain a high. Near Carlen and Myrtle a run-down Italian bakery usually open late doing mob business is closed. Next door the adult video store flashing its throbbing neon sign telling the world that all movies are one dollar; Monday thru Thursday looks empty. As you look up and try to see the real world, but dilapidated projects where squatters claim rights, block the view. The apartments rest on one another like tired brick soldiers. In the middle of all of this disorder an undersized brick building stands with the words "Gospel Church of Christ" painted in bright yellow above the doors and under a cross. A hand written sign taped to the make believe stained glass window in front says "Open 24/7, God never sleeps".

Strangely enough there was only one liquor store in Peers. On this night that the heart of this story took place our main character is seen leaving there.

Along the corner of Hell and Hope an old man with a slight slant to his walk exited the liquor store. He was helped out rather forcefully by a clerk.

"Where closing, go away!"

Sliding down onto the icy street, his feet gradually fell out from under him and he landed with a 'thud' on his ass. The bag securely wrapped in his fist did not move.

"Damn, Libincheese bastard! Can't a person buy a bottle of wine without getting yelled at?" he said as he slowly staggers to his feet. With his cold wrinkled hand he twisted off the cap from the bottle inside the paper bag. The cap plops into slime and breeds in the gutter with hundreds of cigarette butts, H.I.V. dripping-hypodermic needles and soiled Gonorrhea condoms.

He lifted a bottle out of a brown paper bag. "What's the hell did he give me any who? What the hell is this stuff? Lineman's port wine? What the Goddamn is this? I wanted Gallo! Damn!" He glances at a passerby. "Hey, buddy ya gots any change?"

"Get the hell away from me you useless slob!"

"Ya? Same to you! Hey, who you calling slob? I took a shower. Lineman's wine, damn!" He looked around his present surroundings and then at the bottle, reading the label. "Well at least it's a good month."

Drinking the wine down, a smile crossed his face.

"Sure is cold tonight. Damn weather."

The man with a taste for good wine was named Leon. No one knew his real name, just the nickname given to him by the streets. Leon's wife died nine years ago; fire, they said. That apartment right across from where he was standing now was the place that took her life. It was also nine years since Leon's became homeless. Leaning on anyone who would toss him a dollar or two for a bottle. The poor fool would lean on anyone who would make him forget what happened one fiery night nine drunken years ago.

II: Across Town With Joe

"We want our money, Joe!"

"I don't have it! I'll have it soon. I promise!"

"Hey, forget that! We want it now!"

"I don't have it!" Joe Torelli's head fell to the left and then to the right. The fist that moved it around landed one more time on his chin. Drool, merging with blood, ran down his white Armani shirt and tie.

"Let's go for a ride, Joey, okay?"

"Hey, I said I'll have the money soon. I promise!" His quivering voice was ignored.

"Ya, well ya promised that last Friday - get in the car." The Cadillac door opened and Joe against his will went inside.

"Where we goin'?" The car door slammed shut.

III: The Present Tense

The beginning of a cold night blew newspaper and the smell of shit past Leon. His body shook as he sat in a doorway of one of the decaying apartment buildings drinking his port, savoring the drops as they tickled down his throat, sheltering his mind from cold memories.

"Jesus, when's it gonna get warm around here?" Leon said as he closed his eyes and took in a deep breath of cold night air. On the exhale he started singing a song from one of his favorite singers. Leon sang songs when he reached a point of delirium. On most night these words echoed the streets of Peers. You could almost set your watch by them. The drunker he got the louder he sang.

"Well, I say, Hello, Dolly. Hello, Dolly. So nice to see you at the show tonight."

"Hey, shut the hell up down there!" A voice from a near by apartment yelled down.

"Hey, shut up there yourself. Your ruin my Sachmo."

"Hey, Leon, give it a rest!"

"Go back to bed and shut the hell up!" Leon slurred back.

"Leon, I'm gonna come down there and tear you a new asshole in that black ass of yours. Get the hell outta here." Leon rumbled under his breath. The creaking in his tired old bones told him to get up off the curb. Fighting was not in the cards tonight. He wondered aimlessly singing to himself. "Sure is cold. Damn weather."

IV: More Bad Moments For Joe

The black Cadillac with bloody Joe inside traveled east on Waned Avenue crossed, Peers Way and entered into the heart of the Realm. Inside the tinted windows Joe Torelli's crushed nose made a slight whistle when he breathed and his swollen eyes could only made out glimpses of light.

"Forget you guys, you ain't never getting your money!" he mumbled, but the words came out sounding like 'Florgit few fives, sew ain't snever gebin sour smoney!' He could feel his heart beat in his split lips.

A cry he did not know he had in him came out as the man he knew as Flick punched him, again in the eye. Flick's gold nugget and diamond ring exploded Joe's swollen eye like a water balloon dropped from a very tall building.

The other man to the right, known as Stan, took Joe's pinkie finger and put it on the window track of the Cadillac's door. He then raised the window until a crunch sound was heard. Stan then lowered the window and put Joe's ring finger in the track and repeated the punishment until all fingers were compressed. With a slight smile to his acne scared face Stan started on the other hand. Joe contemplated fighting back, but the power it would take to achieve this was beyond him. That little old ant could not move that rubber tree plant. Joe surrendered what little he had left.

V: Peers Wakes Up

The quarter moon gradually removed the coffin lid, awakening the streets of Peers. Figures emerged from dark alleys and stairwells. Whores danced the sacred "Come Fuck Me" dance in the streets and a Cadillac slowed down a dimly lit street. If you where listening from the corner by the ripped open mailbox on Third and Pacific, you could hear low dull moans coming from the Cadillac. Inside five associates and one bloody mess in the backseat looked around to see if the coast was clear.

"Hey, slow down, Frank. This is good enough. Throw him out."

"No sdon't slew fuys!" A slow grousing voice slurred in the back seat.

"Good bye Joe! And I guess this makes you paid in full." The passenger in the front seat nodded his head. The back door opened and, as Joe was being pushed out, Flick stuck a 9" hunting knife (with Laura's D.N.A. on it) into his left side and with little effort the blade came out his back on the right side. Joe did not scream, just bounced and landed along the gutter in front of the Gospel Church of Christ. The Cadillac pulled away at a snail's pace. The men in the car watched and made sure that the Joe did not move.

"Paid in full." One of them said. The Caddy turned right on Seventh Street, leaving yet another creature to suffer in the Realm.

VI: A Warm, Dry Place

Silent in the gutter, Joe tasted sewage water flowing into his swollen mouth. He gagged and then puked; blood and then something that resembled lunch followed. The Lineman's bottle cap came down the gutter, over cigarette butts, leaves and chewing gum and rested on his lip.

After several unspoken minutes Joe moved his head out of the gutter and onto the sidewalk. Tilting his bloated head back he saw the bright yellow cross, hanging on the church's wooden doors.

"Help me, God." He rolled the rest of his body out of the wet cold gutter. Feeble legs inched along as his elbows worked as hands, slithering twelve feet to the wooden church doors.

One of the doors - the right one, had a slight opening. He reached in with his mangled hand, pulling the door open. It took nearly all of his strength to do it. The heat from inside the entry way filled him, giving him enough strength to get to his knees.

VII: Father Leon

Inside the church Joe's frail body shadowed against the outside lights. His head rested on the doorsill. Painfully he looked up. The smell of burning candles and cleanliness filled his crushed sinuses. He was reminded of childhood as he saw pews lined up row after row down to the pulpit. A life-sized crucifix hung behind two pillars. Paint faded walls held pictures of Christ's birth, death and resurrection in all different shapes and hues.

"Excuse me, could you close the door it's a bit cold." Joe looked around and thought he heard a voice.
"Huh?" he responded.

"Hey, boy! You listenin' to me? Close the door, your lettin' the heats gets out." Joe looked around and to his left down the isle of pews a man emerged and looked at him. The reflection of stain glass and lights shining through them made the man looked different: symbolically shaded in red, blues, and greens.

"God?" Joe asked, as he fell on the door handle

shutting it as he hit the floor.

"Lord almighty, what the heck we got here?" Leon took the last swig of his port, looked at the cross, smiled and walked to the door. The man on the floor dripped blood onto everything.

"Hey buddy? Hey man, what happened to yous'?" Leon turned the body over and pulled him a few feet until he tired. There he rested next to this stranger and thought nothing about himself. His head was quiet for the first time in a long time. "Hey, man, wake up. You ain't dead ya still gots' a pulse." A mutilated, swollen face from chin to hairline murmured. Leon had to bend down to him what he was saying.

"Job? Help." Leon wrinkled his forehead, his uncombed gray hair rising a bit.

"Job help? Boy, I ain't the welfare office. Yous' in a church and from the looks of it you might be here again real soon, but in a box."

Joe spoke again, this time slowly. "G - God help me, I don't wanna die." A laugh echoed through the church and Leon hushed himself looking around, mostly at the cross to see if anyone heard him.

"Boy, I sure ain't God. They musts a hit you hard on your head? He chuckled. "Imagine someone mistakin' me for God?"

Joe tried focusing on his surroundings and saw a cross above his head and candles lit to his right. In front of him was a figure: a black man in a black jacket. He shut his blurry swollen eyes and spoke as clear as he could.

"Excuse me, I'm sorry about that, Father." Leon's head wrinkled again and he said nothing this time. But in his mind he laughed. "I went from God to a priest in two minutes. I can live with it."

"Father talk to me, I'm scared. I haven't been to church since I was nine." Leon had a hard time understanding the man, but he listened anyway. "I lost God, Father. And this may sound stupid, but I feel I need him right now. I want to die and know I'm okay."

"Hey, boy, what's your name?"

"Joe, Joseph Torelli."

"Well, Joseph, all you have to do is want to go somewhere else when you die and you will. What ever your last thought is, is where yous' are goin'."

"My thoughts are scattered. With my luck I'll be in Hell."

"Stop talkin' that way boy, or else yous' will go there."

"I borrowed money from some people, Father. Just did it once and couldn't pay them back. Oh, God! It was just nine thousand dollars." Joe tightened his body, just wanting and wanting to cry, yet so unable to. "Father, I don't want to die! I want to live. I'm scared. I want to play with my boy; he's three this month. I want to hug my wife and tell her how special she is." Joe's eyes rolled back into his skull. "I can't feel my legs or hands. Father talk to God, tell him to give me another chance!" Joe's body twitched. His bones cracked, giving up the fight, but his mind was not going to stop the fight. Leon held him, but was afraid to touch him. Everywhere he put his hands blood oozed from injuries only seen in combat.

"Hang in there, Joe. Death ain't so bad. The thing is others peoples death is bad. We don't have to mourn our own death; we just have to accept it. I had a wife once. I tell you if she wasn't the prettiest woman in this entire city. A few years ago, she died on me." Leon's face wrinkled, he wanted so desperately to cry but had forgotten how. "In fire that was - started by the owner of the building. Joseph they torched my home for insurance money. Someone's killed my happiness for a lousy few bucks." Leon's grip on Joe's arm grew tighter. "Of course no ones would say that's what happened, but I heard them talks about it on the streets." Joe sighed a wheezing pain.

"I tried killin' myself by drinkin' to death - that hasn't

worked yet. I tried walkin' in front of cars; they just stop and yell. I tried jumpin' off a roof of a buildin', but I passed out before I did it. Son, I have lived on this earth too long not to die. I envy you. I wish I had the strength to do myself in and forget each and every godforsaken day." Long tears fell from Leon's face. "I just walk these streets, as if I'm doomed never to leave. I can still hear her screamin' I couldn't get to her in time." Leon looked up at the crucifix. "Oh, to be in this poor fool's shoes."

"Father, hold me. I'm so hot. My face is burning up." Leon bent down and laid almost on top of Joe. His body was as cold as ice. Sweat poured off his sliced open forehead, loosening the coagulated blood on top of the wounds. Leon's weather worn hands wiped away the sweat, gentle and delicate. Joe's pulse slowed to almost a stand still and Leon hugged the stranger as if he knew him his whole life. He looked at the cross.

"Damn you! This man has faults, who don't. Leave him be! Leave him alone. Take me! Why won't you let me die? Yous' punish the wrong people" Leon stared into Joe's eyes.

Slowly without much hesitation he spoke. "Father, I'll be okay, wont I? I mean if there really is a God, I guess I'll see him soon - don't ya' think?" His eyes closed, his mumble fainted into a whisper. "Thanks you."

As Leon looked at him he thought he saw a smile come over the swollen face. Joe's lips parted. "Father, why - are - you in the church - so late?" Joe's mind finally gave into his physical condition. His eyes, swollen as they were fluttered like a newborn sparrow spreading its wings for the first time. His chest went in on a last breath and never drew out for another. His arms and legs grew limp.

Leon felt cold chills run through his body. He looked away from Joe and remembered where he was and why he was there. Leon sat up and took the brown paper bag from his inside coat pocket and took a chug of wine.

"Empty!" He groaned. His body grew colder. He stood up to leave and gave Joe the last rights he asked for.

"Joe, maybe yous' in a more comfortable place than I. But, son, I can get honest with ya now since yous' dead. I ain't God and I ain't no priest. I'm just a bum. Just a wino hiding out. Joe, this old buildin' is a safe place, a safe place for everyone. Even if yous' found it five minutes before you die. This is a safe place for an awful lots a people. I just came in this old church for one thing and one thing only. I came in from the cold to get warm and get dry. God Bless you." Leon gave Joe the only possession he had. The empty bottle laid next to the body and Leon looked up at Christ one more time and tipped his head to the cross. He winked and walked down the isle of pews.

His tired old bones carried him out into the cold night air. When he felt it was safe Leon opened the wallet that he had taken from Joe's pocket. "$35, which will get me the Gallo Port, I wanted in the first place and then some." He whistled a famous 'Sachmo' tune from a movie that him and his wife saw on their first date.

Leon buttoned his old coat and tossed the wallet in the gutter. A picture of a young woman holding a baby fell from it and traveled slowly down the streets of Peers.

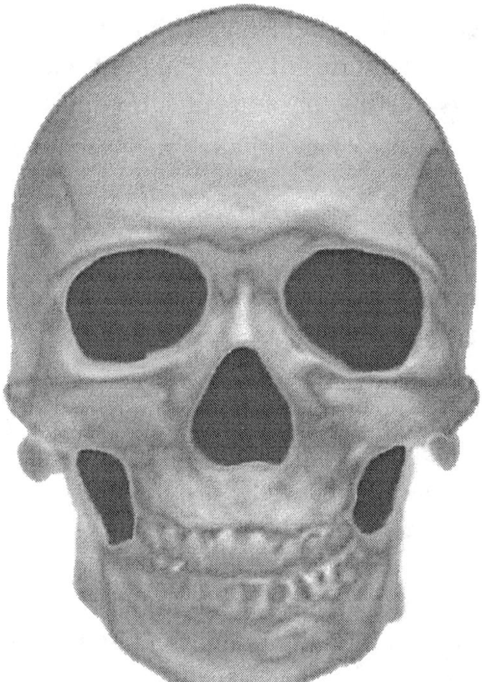

Emily 1

You came to me hidden by silhouetted moon
And left memories of coins on the floor
Even as the time has left - it is my faith
To close my eyes and lock the door - Behind

My security was, at earliest - in voyage
You being such a greater being than I
'Till we lay side by side – black to white
Forgetting how to fear the noose to die

No, I cannot forget such a splendor
As I hide away on moving ship to sea
Still smelling your womanly fragrance
Every where around my stifled me

We dared the greatest taboo of our time
Risking death by noose and trial by brethren
And as the tip of the moon sinks to the sea
I still hold you close with respect and friend

Emily 2

It is unenviable to run from thee
Even the strongest soul cannot hide
Time walks us towards the arms of – He
Crushing everyone with false sense of pride

Gaze beyond your windows ledge
And in attendance you will know
The angels who held your hand
While you struggled to flow

Jesus Christ cannot put aside your - Sympathy
His job was only to acquaint you with
The life you hid from Humanity
While waiting for answers to your uncertainties

"If help and salvation are to come, they can only come from the children, for the children are the makers of men."

Maria Montessori

Little Boy Grape Juice

"I remember Dad telling me to whistle when I was scared. Somehow in some strange way my lips won't stay together. I can't whistle. I'm shaking too much. It's cold out here. My lips won't stop shaking. I can't make a sound. I'm not scared, but I feel so …alone. I've felt alone and scared at the same time before. I don't remember when. I just know I have. But I'm a big boy. I won't cry. Babies who can't find their moms in supermarkets cry that's not me." Blood stopped it's running from the little boy's forehead, into his green eyes, down his swollen mouth; four minutes ago.

"The sun is going down behind the mountain over there. We passed over that mountain, before the car stopped. That mountain seems so far away. But when I reach my hand out to it, I can fit it in my hand like a butterfly. It seems like such a long time ago when we drove over that mountain. But it was just a few minutes ago …I think?

"My head hurts real bad. I can't feel any grape juice running above my eye any more. I know it's grape juice because I can taste the syrupy purple, and the sour after bite of rust. Plus it's leaving a stain on my shirt. Grape juice does that. It leaves a stain on your clothes when you spill. Mom always gives me an upset look when she pulls it out of the washing machine and the stain is still there." The passageway that trickled grape juice above his eye remained stable. Swollen blood -dried - shut eyes attempt to look around.

"I can't see out of my eyes any more. But since the grape juice stopped flowing maybe I can soon." The boy's bruised and sliced hand wiped away dirt and debris from his head. Three of his small fingers slipped into the wound above his eye. The fingers fell in with a moist sloshing sound. Down to the top knuckle. The little boy was reminded of a time his hand got caught in a jelly jar. With a nervous pull his hand slipped out of his wound. The grape juice flowed again.

"I just wiped most of the grape juice off my face with Gwen's shirt. Her brand new shirt my dad just bought for her at the last gas station we stopped at. That was the name of it: The Last Gas Station. The store had a big sign on top of the roof Last Gas and Food for 90 miles. That's what it said. It's the last stop between Hell and the Mojave Desert, that's what my dad told me …before the car started rolling …before I ended up by the bushes." Slowly blood trickled again, down his eye like a tear, onto the crevice of his nostrils, over his swollen upper lip, into his mouth, and dripped dripped down his chin. His shattered body deliberately became cold again as the grape juice flowed; this was how his body reacted to trauma.

"I pumped the gas when we pulled into the gas station.

My mom went to the bathroom with my sister Gwen. Gwen always has to go to the bathroom. My dad went inside and paid for the gas and bought my sister the shirt that I wiped my head with. He bought me a candy bar, I wanted a big 9" hunting knife, dad said I was too young …ut, oh! My head is leaking again …ah, ah, I can't whistle." His voice quivered as the thumping in his head produced tear, tears this time that hurt too much to fall. He tried puckering his swollen lips together, but only a slur came out. His mind was getting that lonely feeling again. One of his swollen eyes broke free from the dried juice. He saw the car again. He just came from the car minutes ago. There was no reason to go back.

"Gwen has collected deer souvenirs since she was eight, that was two years ago. The shirt my dad bought her has a picture of a deer and its baby lying down in the woods. But I ruined it. It has all of the juice I wiped my face with on it. Mom's gonna be mad when she washes it and the stain is still there." The boy tried getting up again. His right leg was twisted and bent behind his back. This made the task of moving an impossible venture. The boy's body from the waist down had no feeling. And he never noticed this when he crawled from the bushes to the car that first time minutes ago; or was it minutes? He never thought why he was in the bushes, or how funny it was that he could not walk. He just wanted to wipe his face so he could see. The boy never felt the agonizing pain of crawling back to the bushes; the safe and scared-free place that he had found. The boy just continued trying to whistle. He only slurred as grape juice fell onto the desert road like ketchup shaken from its bottle.

"I have to sit down for a second. My head's getting dizzy. The sun is going down. It's a real good sun. But it's making me feel scared. The sun usually warms me up when I ride my bike or swim in the ocean. But it's not doing that, it's making me cold" he tried thinking why the sun was cold, his eyes stared right into it "because it's leaving, that's why. Why does it have to leave? Everybody is leaving me. I'm a good boy; don't leave sun. Stay a while and keep me warm." The sun was too far away to hear the boy call him. The sun's job was over for the day. But if the sun did hear the boy call, it would have stayed a few minutes longer, just long enough to warm him up and keep him safe. The sun would never deny a child a warm place to rest.

"I need to get to the tree over there and sleep with my mom. I used to do that when I was a little kid. But, daddy tells me I'm a big boy and I don't have to do that anymore. I can still hear him telling me that. It rained in March (three months ago). I ran into my parents' room and hugged my mom and told her I was scared. My dad woke up, laughing at me. Then he sat me down on his lap and we watched the rain and lightning together. He told me I was old enough to enjoy the rain and not be afraid of it. He said when he was my age he used to go outside and listen to the rain more closely. He liked the rain and lightning after that. It made him fall asleep much faster. So I went back in my room and I opened up the blinds and watched the rain and listened to the thunder. I was a big boy. I like the rain today …but not right now. Right now I'm afraid. And dad is asleep in the car. His head is inside the steering wheel. I tried talking to him, but he was sound asleep.

I tapped him on the shoulder and told him we better get going. All I heard was a gurgling sound coming from his throat. Dad snores a lot when he is sleeping hard. Maybe Dad isn't a big boy today. Maybe he just needs to feel scared and sleep until he feels safe. So I'll let him sleep, I know how that feels. I know because I like sleeping next to Mom. She makes everything okay, like the sun that is gone. But …mom is asleep by the tree and Gwen is too ugly to look at. I got sick when I saw her. I threw up and it burned my throat. That was when I crawled to the car. I crawled on my arms. For some reason my legs are sleeping. I can feel the pins and needles all the way up to my stomach still. It hurts bad when I move. The car door was upside down when I got to it. The tires where still spinning in the air. My Dad's station wagon looked like the cockroach that died in the bathroom last week; all scrunched up and upside down. When Dad wouldn't wake up I grabbed Gwen's shirt with the deer on it. It was in her hand. I took it from her to wipe my head. Gwen is ugly right now." With his one good eye the little boy by the bush looked at the car and the people in it. He watched them sleep, then he looked up and saw the moon sneaking up the other mountain. The one they had yet to reach. He laid on his back and greeted the moon.

"Hello, moon. Did the sun tell you to keep me warm and safe? It wasn't bad to take Gwen's shirt from her, was it? She wasn't using it. And she always lets me play with her toys. But if she needs it, I'll give it back to her." The child rolled over on his stomach. He has rested in the bushes long enough, he thought. But he never thought of his pulse that was falling low as he tried crawling down the bluff towards the tree where his mother slept. He never thought about his sight, the one that was not guiding him. His eyes no longer worked. Something more beautiful than the gift of sight guided him toward his mother - her own warm sun.

"Mom? Mom?" Screaming sounds filled inside him, yet only a whisper was heard, a whisper stuck in a wheeze. "Mommy, I'm cold again. Where's my jacket?" He crawled along the sand, dirt and glass debris. He gripped sticks and gravel with useless clutches, and pulled his body along. He tried whistling. He knew he had to. He thought of a million billion songs to whistle to, but he slurred and coughed on the grape juice that was dripping from his forehead rapidly into his eyes, his mouth. His grip on the sand shot pain to his head, and in his chest he felt an ache. Like the ache he got a little lower in his belly on his birthday. The day he ate the whole box of donuts. He thought of all these things and some things never came to him. But his main thought was mom; to reach the tree where she slept. It didn't matter that he was acting like a baby, wanting and needing so badly. All he wanted was to get warm, and sleep next to his mom. All he needed was to be next to his mom. Since his sun abandoned him minutes ago, his mom would keep him warm. She would never leave her son out in the cold to die. A mother would never deny her son a warm place to rest.

"Mom, wake up! I'm cold Mom. I'm really cold. My head keeps watering, Mom!" His journey down the bluff was ending. Within three feet of him sat his mother. Over and over he reached for his mother's resting body. Over and over his pants that housed his legs which where useless clung to a bush. His pants twisted and twined tighter and tighter onto the limbs of a bush. His tiny blood soaked hands dug deeper into the sand. He pulled and pulled but could not move his body any closer to his mother. The boy lay only a few feet away.

"Mom, wake up, I'm cold. Mom, wake up! When Dad wakes up can we go? I'm still a big boy …mom, ain't I? Look at me, I'm not crying." His feeble arms stretched out his short fingers and added a few more inches closer to his mother. The little boy was still over two feet away. His body shook in spasms and his shredded pants entwined themselves tighter around the branches of the bush. Cold radiated off his mother, and he could feel it on the tips of his fingers. The little boy never felt the cold from his mother, though. No, the little boy felt heat, and he knew that was love enough to keep him warm until she woke up.

"Mom, when are we going to get to Uncle Pete's house?" No answer came from his mother. The little boy smiled and finally gave up the struggle of freeing his legs.

"Okay, Mom just sleep, I'll be quiet. Just get some sleep. I understand." The boy dropped his head onto the cooling desert ground. He placed his lips together and finally whistled in the dark. Without a slur or wheeze he whistled like a sparrow on a warm spring day. He kept on whistling until the grape juice from his forehead stopped flowing, and his body stopped trembling.

"It will be alright Mom, Dad will wake up soon. We'll all leave together …the whole family."

The little boy with grape juice for blood quietly stopped moving. He remained inches away from the warmest spot on earth: his mother's heart.

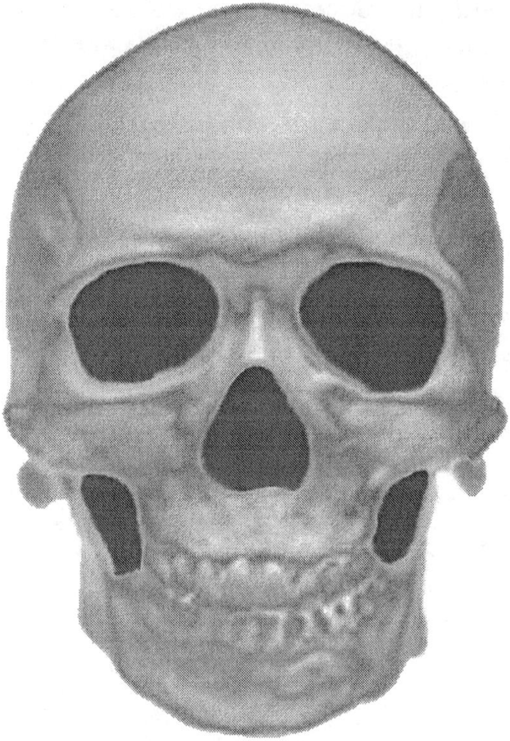

Emily 3

Peer of the realm attached to lumber
For speaking certainty to those around
The downfall was the way he - slumber

He carried the albatross on his back -
In front of missionary and adversary
Very weary was his frame of mind -
Very encouraged were his deceivers

He who cast the first stone shall be - Jew
The lie told within a book of divinity
The first stone was cast by - Father
Who allowed his son to drag his sorrow

Our lord - the infatuated - Muchausen by proxy
Summoned - death onto his next of kin
To conceal - the truth about adoring a whore

The Killing Mind

The Stranger-

The Mall-

The Ritual

The Process

The Drill Origin-

Behind The Mall-

Inside The Mall-

About The Author

John Turi has been writing fiction and poetry since he was nine weeks within the womb. He would scrawl *Haikus* on the uterus and recite prose while his mom slept. Away from writing (which is rare), John is an avid collector of fine literature, autographs and ephemera. The Turi library consists of hundreds of rare books and important works of art spanning more than 400 years. He resides in Southern California with his wife, three cats (two who do not get along and the other who's gay) and two dogs (who are his best friends). John is currently contemplating his next novel as he hides in his home, under a desk, smoking old cigarette butts from an ashtray, while crying like a baby with Colic.